EPISODES

JOSHUA S. TOMMASO

For information regarding permission, please write to:
info@barringerpublishing.com
Barringer Publishing, Naples, Florida
www.barringerpublishing.com

Design and layout by Linda S. Duider
Cape Coral, Florida

ISBN: 978-1-954396-07-4
Library of Congress Cataloging-in-Publication Data
Episodes / Joshua Tommaso

Printed in U.S.A.

CONTENTS

EPISODE ONE

"Elaine, are you going to get out of bed today, or do I need to have Cathy watch over Steven again?" Joe asked, frustrated and staring at Elaine, hoping that her response will be more than just a simple yes. It had been several weeks since Elaine has watched their young son for a whole day. The past month, Elaine had just been laying around the house, not talking much and letting herself go. Her usual beauty is cloaked in a dirty robe; her blond hair is now matted in knots, greasy, and is like a bird's nest. Normally, her blue eyes sparkle with a sweet tranquility that can light up a room, but lately, it seems like the light behind her eyes had burned out. Elaine had seemed off to Joe, but to him it was just a simple bout of depression. Maybe the responsibilities of being a mother the past four years are catching up to her or she is having late postpartum. Elaine does a great job of taking care of Steven when she is well, but she has not been doing that. The next-door neighbor, Cathy, has been watching their son while Elaine is incapacitated.

"No, no!" Elaine said, staring at the white wall from her bed.

Joe, a little surprised that she said no instead of yes,

thought that maybe now she was getting better. He still felt something was off though; she said no, yet, she was staring off into space, as if not entirely acknowledging him.

"Are you sure; I can ask Cathy to watch Steven, he loves to play with Zack and Katy, especially since they are all so close in age," Joe said as he walked to the kitchen to get a large thermos and began to fill it with water.

"I can watch Steven; I need to protect him," Elaine said from the bedroom.

"Protect him?" Joe said a little confused. He walked back to the bedroom.

"Yes," Elaine said while getting out of bed.

Joe was surprised to see her emerge from the bed. She had not moved out of it other than to go to the bathroom and back. He thought that is what she was going to do, but he was surprised to see that she was walking to the closet.

"Are you going to go take a shower?" Joe asked, going back to the kitchen so he could put ice into his thermos. Afterward, he went to the kitchen cabinet next to the sink that held his spirits.

"Yes," was all Elaine said.

When she heard the liquor cabinet opened, she darted her head towards the doorway.

"Joe, are you drinking again this early in the morning?" she yelled.

She sounded furious, the first real emotion from her in weeks. Joe, startled, yelled back.

"Oh no, this is for later, I'm just mixing it up for later in the day after work; the thermos will keep it cold till I get off work."

He blushed, wondering how she knew he was mixing his whiskey and water together. He thought she didn't notice, lying in bed motionless the past couple of weeks. She seemed to be much more observant than he thought. Now, he wonders if she knew he was lying. Who would mix a drink this early for later in the day?

"Anyways, what do you mean by you are going to protect Steven?" Joe said, as he walked towards the bathroom, watching Elaine undress then hop into the shower.

"It's like I said, Joe; I have to protect him," she said in a monotone voice.

Now, Joe was confused. Earlier, she had a sound of emotion—it was an angry one, but it was a form of an emotion; now it sounds as if it left her again.

"I know," Joe said starting to get a little agitated.

"What do you mean by it, what are you going to protect him from? Is there something I don't know about?"

"I'm his mother, it is my job to protect him; I have a sudden urge to be protective of him, that is all, okay?"

She still sounded monotone, but Joe was surprised that she has been speaking more than just a few words at a time. This time she responded in full sentences. However, he still felt something was off, her speech was strange, and he just couldn't seem to pinpoint it. Suddenly, he heard a soft cry come from Steven's room.

Steven was up in his bed, wide awake and jumping happily. His cry was not out of sadness or anger, it was his awakening cry to get attention from his parents, or more so lately, his father.

"Hey, little guy, you awake?" Joe asked while looking at his son's blue eyes. He takes his eyes from his mother, sparkling blue, glistening in the morning sun, beaming through the window. Joe then began to run his hands through his son's soft, light, brown hair. The warmth from the sun coming from the window warmed up Steven's hair; it felt nice in Joe's fingers and reminded him of freshly dried laundry.

"Dad, am I going to play?"

Joe was expecting to say yes—yes, he was going to see Cathy today, but Elaine wanted to watch Steven.

"No, mommy is going to watch you today. You will play with mommy today, okay? Maybe later she will let you go play with Zack and Katy, does that sound okay?"

"Mommy?"

Steven was confused within his three-year-old self, he was used to getting up, getting dressed, and going next door to play, till his dad came back from work.

"Yes, Steven, mommy is going to watch you today; she is getting ready right now. Matter of fact, let's get you ready for mommy."

Joe then walked over to the dresser and got out some clothes for Steven. He got his son's favorite Power Rangers shirt, blue jean shorts, and New York Yankee's baseball cap, just like the one he wears. Then Joe put on Steven's favorite light up sneakers and got him out of bed.

"Light up shoes!" Steven said happily while stomping around the room watching the lights flash.

Again, and again, Steven would stomp his feet and yell "light up shoes, light up shoes!"

Joe loved his son very much and felt bad that he had to work long hours. Joe was the general manager of a local steak house and often did not get home, till late in the evening. He did not get to spend much time with his son. Joe always told himself that one of these days he would take Steven out to go fishing . . . one of these days.

"Daddy, I'm hungry," Steven said rubbing his belly.

"I'm sorry, Steven, I forgot to make you something this morning—how about cereal?"

"Cereal, cereal!" Steven said happily, jumping up and down excitedly.

Usually, Joe made Steven an egg sandwich, with a glass of milk, but he did not have time this morning, especially since Elaine surprised him by actually getting up this morning and conversing with him more than usual. Joe got the cereal and milk together and handed it to his son.

"Thanks, Daddy," Steven said while keeping his eyes on the bowl the whole time.

"You're welcome, Son," Joe said smiling. Then, out of the corner of his eye, he saw Elaine walk across the room next to the kitchen.

"Elaine," Joe said quickly.

"You going to say high to Steven?"

Elaine just kept walking towards the bedroom not saying anything.

"Mommy," Steven yelled, with excitement. He hadn't seen his mother walking around in weeks, usually he saw her confined in bed but it was a surprise to see his mom walking about.

"Don't worry, Steven, I'll be out to protect you in a bit." Elaine said from the bedroom.

"Protect me! Protect me!" Steven said, repeating the words.

Those words echoed in Joe's ear; he did not like the word "protect" this morning. It seemed ominous to him; what was Elaine trying to protect Steven from? Is she having a sudden urge to protect him in a nurturing way? Elaine has been confined to bed for almost a whole month and had not interacted with Steven the whole time. Maybe she really does have a motherly instinct to protect him. Joe didn't know, but he just still didn't feel right about it.

"Elaine, you sure you don't want Cathy to watch Steven today?"

"Cathy!" Steven chirped, standing in his chair.

"I'll protect Steven!" Elaine yelled from the bedroom.

Joe left it alone. Frustrated, he walked over to the counter where his thermos sat, grabbed it, and took a swig from it.

"Okay, okay, I get it, you'll protect Steven," Joe mumbled to himself.

Something inside told him to take Steven across the street to Cathy's, but Joe really wanted to see Elaine be productive rather than just lay around all day. Joe decided to finish up and leave for work, then suddenly Elaine emerged from the bedroom in some old, black sweats and a dirty, grey t-shirt. Joe was perplexed; she laid around for weeks and looked grungy, then today, she took a shower then dressed in grungy clothes. Before he said something, Elaine answered his question.

"I'm going to clean today; I have a sudden urge to get the house clean," Elaine said, sounding chipper all of a sudden.

Joe was set aback; he wondered where this Elaine had come from. One minute she seemed unaware, then she got angry and now she is chipper like she was her old self again, in a matter of half an hour. Joe was conflicted; he was happy that Elaine seemed to be getting better, yet something was nagging him. It didn't seem right for her mood to change that quickly. He thought it over and decided that, before going to work, he would drop by Cathy's.

"That's great, the house does need some cleaning up." Joe looked around.

It was true, the house was a mess. Elaine always did the cleaning; Joe never had time to do anything around the house. He worked six days a week, usually ten to twelve hours a day and when he returned, he would eat dinner. Lately, he would bring food home from work, since Elaine hadn't been cooking. Then afterwards, he drank his whiskey and water mix and watched the news or sports till he fell asleep. On days off, he was too tired to do any housework, drank the day away and watched news or sports all day. The process repeated itself every week.

"I'll have Steven help me clean today," Elaine said while going to the kitchen to grab some cleaning supplies.

"Clean! Clean!" Steven said happily.

"You excited to clean little man?" Joe said smiling, this was the first time in a while Joe was feeling a glimmer of happiness thinking that maybe some normality was returning. And he was happy to have a clean home again.

"Okay, Steven, daddy has to go to work; you be a good boy and help mommy clean the house, okay? I'll be back tonight."

Joe bent down and gave his son a hug, grabbed his thermos, then headed towards the door.

"Oh, Elaine, if you feel like cooking tonight, call me at work this evening and let me know; if I don't get a phone call, I'll just bring some food from work again."

Joe waited for a reply but received no answer.

"Did you hear me?" Joe said a little agitated.

"Yes," is all Elaine said, then she started to clean.

Joe left shaking his head.

Joe stepped outside and saw that clouds were beginning to form, and the sun was slowly fading behind the newly formed, white curtain. He then took a swig from his thermos and placed it in his 86' Dodge Ram. He was proud of that truck. He bought it brand new eight years ago when he got the General Manager's job at the Black Steer Steak House; it was the first brand new vehicle he had ever bought. Usually, he was too poor to afford a new one, so he always purchased beat-up cars that would last a couple of years, then he would sell and buy another. Normally, he would get half of what he paid originally, so getting the next one wasn't as big of a hit. This truck he treated with great care. Even though he was busy with work, he always managed to get regular maintenance for it; he usually went on his lunch breaks or on his day off when he wasn't too tired or drinking too much. Before he closed the door, he grabbed some mints from the glove box and popped about three or four into his mouth and headed over to Cathy's house.

Cathy heard a knock on her door. She expected that it would be Joe dropping off Steven for the day; she answered the door with a big smile. Cathy was surprised to see just Joe. "Where's Steven? Is there something wrong with him?" she asked a little worried.

She enjoyed having Steven over; her son and daughter loved having him over to play all day. Joe looked at Cathy, her dark, curly, brown hair draped slightly over her shoulders. She was a fairly large woman, but the nicest person anyone would ever meet; she loved children and truly enjoyed having Steven over. Joe felt guilty that she had to watch him for nearly a month, but he was happy to let her know that today she didn't have to for once.

"No, Steven is doing great."

"Oh, how's Elaine doing?"

"That's the thing; she got out of bed today and said that she will be watching him today."

Joe darted his eyes a bit, he didn't want to tell Cathy about how Elaine said she will protect Steven—he didn't want to bring it up.

"Well, that's great! I'm glad she is doing well enough to watch Steven today, hopefully she'll keep getting better," Cathy said with a smile that matched her sparkling brown eyes.

"Yes, me too."

"Well, is that why you came over, just to let me know that Steven won't be over today?"

Cathy felt there was something more that Joe was not telling her.

"Well, there is that," Joe said. "But I was wanting to ask you if maybe you can check on them later today, maybe around lunch time? Elaine didn't seem one hundred percent, and I just want to make sure that she is doing okay with Steven and that he had lunch and what not, if you don't mind, that is."

He felt a little worried that maybe she would become suddenly busy for the day, since she didn't have to watch Steven. He could ask Danny who lived next to Joe, but he didn't want to bother him.

"Yeah, I can do that, is there something wrong still?" Cathy looked into Joe's almond brown eyes that matched his tanned, Italian skin.

"No, it's just this is the first day that Elaine has been up and about in over a month and I just want to make sure she doesn't relapse then decide to lay around all day and not take care of Steven."

"Okay, I understand. I'll check in on them around noon and give you a call at work to give you an update."

"Okay, thanks, I really appreciate it. Please call me no matter what, good or bad, I just want to make sure Steven is okay."

"I will, I understand," Cathy said smiling.

"Okay, well must get to work, have a great day."

Joe then turned around and walked off. Cathy closed the door.

Drinking early in the morning again, Cathy thought to herself shaking her head. *Yet, he does deeply care for his son.* Then she walked to the kitchen to make breakfast for her kids.

Joe walked back to his truck and was about to leave, but he decided to check on Elaine and Steven really quick; he just wanted some reassurance before he left. He walked up to the window and peaked in and saw that Elaine was cleaning, or something similar to it. He saw a big pile of clothes in bags in the middle of the living room. He opened the door and saw Elaine dragging another bag from the bedroom and throwing it on top of the pile.

"Everything okay?" he said, looking at the pile of bags; he was only gone for about fifteen minutes and was surprised to see a pile this big in the middle of the room.

"Yes, everything is fine. Oh, why did you go to Cathy's, I told you I'm going to be protecting Steven today."

The word "protect" stung Joe once again; he was growing a little tired of that word and wished she would stop using it. Instead, he took a deep breath and told her a white lie.

"I was just letting her know she didn't have to watch Steven today since you will be pro . . . err, I mean, watching Steven today. I didn't want her to worry. I felt that if I didn't let her know, I'm sure she would have been curious as to why I didn't bring him over today."

He almost said the word protect himself casually. It was starting to get to him, so he decided to go ahead and leave. It looked like Elaine was cleaning like she said, no matter how unusual it was, but before he left, he had to ask.

"Why are you putting all of the clothes in black bags and piling them in the living room?"

"Because I'm cleaning," Elaine said, walking to the kitchen. Opening the cabinets and taking the dishes out that rattled and clanged as she set them on the counter.

"What are you doing now?" Joe asked peaking around the kitchen doorway.

"I'm cleaning, don't worry, I have to put everything in a pile, so I can properly sort everything later. Now go, I will protect Steven and clean the house." Then she went back to taking the dishes out of the cabinets.

Joe looked at his watch and realized it was 8:40 a.m. "Okay, I need to head to work. If you need anything, call me, okay?" There was no reply.

Then it hit Joe. "Where is Steven?" A little worried, he asked because he hadn't seen him.

"Here I am, Daddy!" Steven came running out of his room with a pile of toys in his arms. "Mommy told me to take all my toys and throw them on top of this pile," he said, with a childish glee.

"Oh." Joe was a little confused, he has never seen anyone clean like this before, but at least Elaine was being productive and Steven seemed happy helping his mother, so Joe went to give his son another hug then walked out of the front door. Joe got into his truck, took a drink, started the engine and headed off to work. *I hope today will be a good day*, he thought to himself; he just didn't feel comfortable about the situation, but he needed to get to work. Joe checked his watch again.

"I am going to be late if I don't hurry." Then Joe sped down the road while taking yet another swig out of his thermos.

Steven was now alone with his mother. Elaine's mood seemed to be slowly reversing downhill after Joe left. When he left, she seemed to be in a happier mood and almost seemed to be back to her old self, but now she was slowing down. In her defense, she did grab dozens of bags worth of clothes, dishes, and other oddities from around the house and piled it all into the center of the living room. Steven started calling it bag mountain. Steven looked at it with mischievous eyes. He then looked at his mother who was standing by the front living room window staring off into the street. She did not move, so he took his chance and dived onto bag mountain. Steven jumped from one bag to another and eventually reached the top. He was happy with this accomplishment and started to jump up and down with glee shouting "I'm on the top, I'm on the top!"

Steven continued to jump up and down happily. "Mommy, look at me, I'm on top!" Elaine just stood there, staring out of the window. She was muttering something under her breath, but Steven could not hear what she was saying.

"Mommy! Mommy!" he kept squealing; he was desperately trying to get his mother's attention. Still, she stood there, unmoved, like a statue—just staring out of the window muttering quietly to herself. Slowly, gradually, her muttering began to grow louder. Soon Steven could make out what she was saying.

"I'll protect him, you can never have him, I'll protect him, you can never have him." Elaine just stood there, still un-moved. Her chanting began to grow louder, and louder . . . then silence. As soon as the chanting started to gain momentum, she stopped.

"Mommy, you okay?" Steven stopped jumping on top of his little mountain and looked at his mother. He could understand the sentence his mother was saying, but he did not know what she meant. "Protect, protect, is a monster coming mommy?" he said laughing. He thought it was a game she was playing, he thought it was a make-believe game like the ones he and his friends next door would play. So, he began to play along.

"Oh no, Mommy, the monster's got me." Then in a blink of an eye his mom turned around and stared at him, with fire in her eyes. She hissed out loudly "I'll protect him, you can never have him!" She began to yell at the top of her lungs and rushed towards Steven like a momma lion protecting her cub. Steven began laughing, thinking that his mother was playing along.

"Help me, help me," Steven said giggling. Then suddenly, Elaine rushed to Steven and pushed him off the top of the bag pile, screaming "Leave him alone, I'll protect him, you can't have him." Saliva was sprinkling out of her mouth and hitting Steven.

"Oh, Mommy. That hurt," Steven began to utter a cry.

Elaine looked over at Steven then snapped her head back. "You hurt my son, you cannot have him, I swear you can never have him!" She began to claw at the air. Steven now couldn't tell if his mom was still playing or not. She had never pushed him like that before. Then looking at his mom clawing at the air, he yelled in his childlike voice, "Mommy, we can stop playing," but Elaine kept clawing at the air, screaming, "You can never have him, I'll protect him."

Steven was growing scared. "Mommy, we don't have to play anymore. You are scaring me." Steven got up to walk towards his mom, but she ignored him, still yelling, clawing, thrashing around, as if there was something there.

As Steven approached closer, he could see that his mom's eyes were fixed straight ahead. He thought maybe there was someone really there, but he could tell there wasn't. The wall was right in front of Elaine. He asked his mom with a trembling voice, "Mommy are we still playing?" There was no response. Then Steven came up to his mom and pulled on her shirt. Suddenly, she stopped and looked down at Steven.

"Don't worry, I'll protect you. He will not hurt you."

"Who, Mommy? Are we still playing?"

"Don't you see him? He is standing right here, I've been fighting him off the whole time, keeping him away from you. Now go, run!" Then Elaine started to slash at the air again and was breathing heavily.

"Mommy, there's no one there. We can stop playing now." Steven was beginning to get scared and was lightly shaking all over. Then Elaine, fast as lightening, turned to Steven and yelled at him at the top of her lungs, "Go Steven, this is not a game, this demon is trying to take you away from me."

"Demon?" Steven asked.

He was growing more scared by the minute. He had heard about demons but knew that they were not real. He was confused and looked at his mom. Steven was trying to decide if his mom was playing, or that she really thought there was something there; he almost believed something was there too.

"I said run, Steven," his mother yelled. Steven stood still, he was frightened, he didn't know what to do. He did not see anyone there, and his mom's actions were affecting him. "Steven, go, he is going to kill you!" Steven froze. He heard the word kill and froze. Elaine then turned around and grabbed Steven. "This demon has frozen you with his stare, I'll protect you!" She grabbed Steven in her arms and then ran to his room. She looked around with hysterical eyes and under her breath, she whispered to Steven, "Don't worry, I'll protect you, I'll hide you from the demon, he will never find you."

She spotted the closet door. Elaine took Steven to the closet and put him in it. After she closed the door, she took his bed and put it in front of the door. Then she grabbed the dresser and moved it in front of the bed for extra measure. "Don't worry, he'll never find you in there. I've blocked the door, you are safe. I'll fight him away." Then Elaine walked out of the bedroom.

Steven heard his bedroom door close. He was scared, tears began to roll down his cheeks. He realized this was not part of the game. It was dark, very dark. The bed and dresser kept the light from filtering under the crack of the door. Steven's heart began to race, and his tears began to come more rapidly, and before he knew it, he was bawling, screaming, "Mommy, Mommy, let me out."

Several minutes passed and there was no trace of his mom in the bedroom. After several more minutes of yelling and crying, he soon began to calm down. He stopped not only because he was growing tired of it, but because he could hear his mother in the living room, screaming, throwing stuff around. He heard dishes breaking, the sound of broken pieces scattering across the wall. Steven laid over on his side and began to softly cry, but no tears came out this time, there were none to be shed. He closed his eyes and hoped this was just a nightmare.

Cathy was finishing up making lunch for Katy and Zack.

Zack was playing his Super Nintendo in the living room and Katy was playing with some Barbie dolls next to the TV.

"Guys, lunch is ready." Zack paused his game and ran into the kitchen.

"Katy, are you hungry?"

"No Mommy, I'm busy helping Barbie get ready for her shopping spree."

Cathy smiled to herself; she enjoyed watching her daughter play. She looked at Katy's dark brown, curly hair and it reminded her how much her daughter reminded her of herself. Zack came running in the kitchen. "What's for lunch?" he asked smiling. Zack was a little overweight, like his mother, but he was very active for his age. He was only playing video games because Steven wasn't over today. Usually, they were outside playing tag or catch. Zack was three years older than Steven, but he viewed Steven as a little brother. Since he had only a little sister, he grew pretty close to Steven. "I've got macaroni and cheese ready," Cathy looked at Zack expecting his face to light up because it was his favorite.

"With ketchup?" he said smiling.

"Yes, honey, with ketchup." Then she walked over to the fridge and grabbed a bottle of ketchup for Zack.

"Katy, you sure you don't want to eat?"

"No, Mommy, I'm still playing." Katy was Steven's age, around three and a half, and Katy smiled shaking her head sighing, "Kids, you got to love them."

"Mom, will Steven be over tomorrow?" Zack said while squeezing a glob of ketchup onto his mac and cheese.

"I don't know, it depends on if Joe wants me to or not."

Then it hit her, she realized it was past noon and she was supposed to go check on Steven and Elaine after lunch.

"Speaking of Steven, I have to go and check on them."

"Can I come?" Zack asked, after swallowing two spoonful's of noodles.

"No, I can do it myself, it won't take long."

"Oh, okay. I'll go back and play my game."

Okay, honey, look after your sister."

"Don't worry, I think she will be okay, she's still playing with her dollies," Zack said poking fun at his sister. Katy either didn't hear or bother, or just simply ignored him.

"I won't take long, you stay in the house and do not go anywhere, I'll just be next door for a couple of minutes and be back. Zack don't forget . . ."

"I know, I know, don't go out of the house."

"And?" Cathy said winking at her son.

"Don't answer the door to strangers." Then Zack went back to his Super Nintendo and began to play his game again. Katy still played with her Barbie's, peacefully ignoring the world around her.

Cathy headed across the street. She noticed that the clouds were growing darker and that the smell of rain filled the air. She walked up the steps and knocked on the door. There was no answer. She knocked again and still there was no answer. Cathy saw Elaine's car in the driveway, so she knew Elaine must be home, unless maybe she took Steven on a walk. She knocked one more time to see if anyone would come to the door—still no answer. Looking to her side she noticed that the blinds were open, so she walked towards the window and decided to take a peek just to make sure. Lifting her hands up to her forehead she looked inside. To her amazement, she saw a large pile of black trash bags in the middle of the living room. "Is she cleaning?" she whispered to herself. "If so, that is a weird way to clean." Staring into the room she did not see anyone. Then, when she was about to turn around to leave, she noticed in the corner of her eye that Elaine had emerged from the kitchen. Cathy smiled and began to knock on the window, hoping that Elaine would see her. After knocking, she expected Elaine to see her and come open the door, but she did not. Elaine began to pace back and forth. She was talking loudly to herself but Cathy could not make out what Elaine was saying. "Elaine, Elaine, open the door, it's me Cathy." Still, Elaine was pacing back and forth, back and forth, ignoring everything around her.

Cathy walked to the door and knocked as loud as she could. No one came to the door, she began to worry because she thought that if Elaine didn't open the door, surely Steven would have. Cathy pounded on the door yelling at Elaine. "Open the door, I'm here to check on you and Steven, to make sure you are okay." Growing frustrated, Cathy walked back to the window, hoping that this time Elaine or Steven would hear her. Yet, Elaine was still pacing back and forth as if nothing was going on. Cathy could still see that Elaine was talking to herself. She began to feel uncomfortable; she was going to run back home and call Joe to let him know what was going on. She looked back at her house, thinking about what to do. She turned around to try one more time, but when she did, Elaine's face was staring back at Cathy through the window.

Cathy screamed in surprise. "Elaine, you scared the crap out of me!" Elaine didn't say anything, she just stared at Cathy, mumbling something to herself that Cathy could not hear.

"Elaine, let me in, I'm here to check on you and Steven." Elaine looked at Cathy through the window; she looked angry—Cathy began to grow even more uncomfortable. "Please answer the door." She then walked to the door and tried to open it, but it was locked. She looked over at the window and saw that Elaine was gone. Cathy began trying the doorknob, turning, pulling, jiggling it, but it was no use—it was locked. She started to pound on the door and suddenly the door flew open. Elaine was standing there, motionless, whispering to herself. "Elaine, are you okay? I could see that you were talking, but I could not hear what you were saying." Elaine was still softly mumbling to herself, there was fire in her eyes, and she stared at Cathy with tremendous hate.

Steven heard the pounding at the front door, and he heard muffled voices. He could not tell if it was just his mom, or maybe his dad was home. Steven began to yell, "Mommy, Mommy, let me out!" Cathy heard the cries coming from across the living room. "Elaine, where is Steven?" Elaine looked at Cathy and then back at where the crying was coming from, then she looked back at Cathy and yelled at the top of her lungs, "I'll protect him, you can never have him" then she lunged at Cathy trying to grab her throat. "What the . . ." Cathy was startled, she moved to the side narrowly dodging Elaine's lunge. "Elaine, what are you doing? It's me, Cathy, I'm just . . ." and before she could finish her sentence Elaine came running at her. "To take my son! I'll never let you have him!"

Cathy ran back into the house and shut the door behind her.

"Mommy, Mommy, let me out, please!"

"Steven, is that you?" Cathy heard the cry coming from the bedroom; she ran into Steven's room and heard the cries coming from behind the closet door, blocked by the dresser and bed.

"Steven, it's me, Cathy, I'll come get you." Cathy was shocked to see the bed and dresser in front of the door, and why was he locked up in there?

As soon as Cathy began to move the dresser, Elaine came charging into the bedroom. "You can't have him you demon!" Elaine rushed at Cathy, she dodged and looked around the room for something to fend off Elaine. Elaine was smaller than Cathy, but she was agile and fast. Cathy spotted a lamp on the floor and grabbed it, and when Elaine came around for another attack, Cathy hit her across the face with the lamp; the light bulb made a popping noise and Elaine howled—a howl that sounded haunting. Elaine covered her eyes, momentarily dazed by the shattered light bulb fragments and the sudden attack. Cathy took advantage of this delay and quickly moved the dresser, then she was beginning to push the bed when Elaine began to regain her senses. "Leave him alone, demon!" Cathy got the bed moved and opened the closet door. She saw Steven laying on his side crying. He couldn't open his eyes he was so scared. Cathy bent over and grabbed him. Suddenly, Elaine charged and Cathy couldn't move fast enough, with Steven in her arms. Elaine grabbed Cathy by the throat and she let go of Steven.

"Steven, run next door, hurry!" Steven was frozen solid; he

was paralyzed with fear. Cathy was surprised at the strength of Elaine; she did not look like she would have this kind of strength, as she was so much smaller than Cathy. One last time, Cathy managed to yell out "Steven, run to my house, now!" Steven snapped back to his senses, he saw his mom chocking Cathy and couldn't comprehend what was going on, but he listened. He got up and ran; he ran as fast as he could, crying, crying and not looking back. He ran next door and sat on Cathy's porch. He didn't want Zack or Katy to see him like this.

"You can't have him, demon!"

"Elaine, Steven is gone!"

"What?" Elaine's rage was so focused on Cathy, she did not realize that Steven was gone.

"You killed him, didn't you!" Elaine began to tighten her grip on Cathy's throat. Cathy was having a hard time breathing. She didn't know what to do, Elaine was too strong. Suddenly, Cathy saw a shard of glass from the bulb laying on the dresser. It must have flown on top of it; luckily for her it was within reach and she didn't have to bend down. Cathy did not want to kill Elaine, but just hurt her enough to make her let go. Cathy grabbed the shard and ran it across Elaine's right top hand. She screamed and let go of Cathy; Cathy took this moment and ran towards the living room.

"You shall not leave, demon!" Then, Elaine lunged at Cathy like a tiger, she must have leapt ten feet. Cathy was once again surprised at what Elaine could physically accomplish.

Elaine caught Cathy by the leg and they both came crashing to the ground. Cathy began kicking at Elaine, trying to get out of her tight grasp. Elaine kept yelling, screaming, trying to climb onto Cathy to get to her. "I will kill you, demon!" Cathy kept kicking Elaine in the face, but she kept coming, then Elaine was on top of Cathy but Cathy rolled over with Elaine and now Cathy was on top of Elaine bear hugging her. "Help! Help!" Cathy yelled at the top of her lungs, hoping someone would hear her pleas. They kept struggling, but Cathy was bigger than Elaine. Elaine wriggled out of her shirt and slinked from under Cathy. Elaine was not wearing a bra and was completely topless. Elaine got up and was about to jump back on top when Cathy grabbed Elaine by the pants and Elaine fell down. Elaine was wearing sweats and managed to shed off her pants; now she was completely naked. Cathy accidently took Elaine's underwear and now Elaine was naked, yelling, screaming a horrible screech that Cathy would never forget.

"I'll kill you, demon!" Cathy got up and ran out of the front door. Cathy ran across the street screaming at Steven to get in the house. "Steven, I told you to get in the house, get in the house now!" Steven saw Cathy running towards him and he saw his mother chasing after Cathy, naked. Steven's eyes grew wide, he had never seen his mom naked before and was embarrassed and scared. Steven got up and ran to the door, but it was locked. "Steven, yell for Zack or Katy to open the door, quick!" Cathy was just crossing into her yard, Elaine tripped on the curb. "Hurry, Steven!" Steven started pounding on the door and yelled for Zack and Katy.

Zack was playing his video game when he heard the pounding and screaming at the front door. He paused the game and looked out of the window. He saw his mom running up the walkway and saw Elaine naked lying on the ground, blood all over her hands and screaming. Soon, Elaine got up and began chasing after Cathy. Zack ran to the door and opened it, Steven came rushing in and Cathy soon followed. Cathy shut the door right when Elaine made it up the stairs. Cathy locked the door and called 911.

Elaine was pounding on the door, screaming, scratching at the door. Steven heard the scratches, it sounded like when Kit-Kat, Zack's and Katy's dog, wanted in the house. The screaming pierced Steven; it was more of a screeching scream. "Yes, police, I need assistance, my neighbor is trying to kill me, she thinks I'm a demon . . . yes, that's right, I'm not joking." Then Cathy held the phone towards where the screaming was coming from. "Yes, that's right, 1228 Artzer St., please hurry." Cathy looked for the kids.

"Steven, Zack, Katy, come here now!" Cathy took the kids to the kitchen, which was in the back of the house. She was trying to keep the kids from hearing the heart-wrenching screams, but it was no use, the screams penetrated the house— the whole neighborhood could hear Elaine's bloodcurdling screams. Soon, there were people coming out of their houses wondering what was going on. What everyone saw was Elaine pounding on Cathy's front door, naked, and screaming, "Let me in, you demon! You can't have him!"

Soon the police arrived. When dispatch told them what was going on, they didn't believe it, but dispatch was right, there really was a naked woman, covered in blood, banging on someone's front door. They got out and approached Elaine.

"Ma'am, is everything okay?" They approached slowly; they could tell that Elaine was mentally ill. She turned around and saw the two officers approaching. She hissed at them, then Elaine charged. "Grab her low and I'll grab her high," the officer yelled to his partner. When she charged at them, the first officer grabbed her by the waist, then the second officer came in and held her, wrapping himself around her shoulders. Soon, all three fell to the ground. Meantime, Cathy remembered she should call Joe and let him know what was happening. "Hello, Joe? Yeah, this is Cathy. You are not going to believe this."

She was right, Joe did not believe her at first. Yet, he knew something was not right this morning. He hung up the phone and let everyone know at work there was a family emergency. Joe got into his truck, dug under his seat and took out his thermos. Joe took a gulp, then another and then another; he wiped his lips and sighed. While hiding the thermos back under his seat, he popped in a handful of mints and drove home, cursing under his breath.

It began to rain, and thunder echoed in the sky. Flashes of lightning illuminated the dark, ominous clouds. Joe arrived home and saw the cops putting Elaine in the back of a cruiser. She was screaming, fighting back at the cops, bloody, wet, and completely naked. He didn't believe what he saw. He grabbed a couple more mints and popped them in when he saw the cops close the doors and began walking towards the house. He got out of the truck and talked to the cops. The cops knew some of the story, but not all. After giving his information to the officers, he walked to Cathy's house to get Steven and hear the full story from Cathy, since she witnessed it and was involved in nearly all of it.

Cathy told Joe everything and he was shocked; he had been with Elaine for five years and had never seen her have an episode. Steven ran up to Joe and hugged him crying into his dad's waist,

"Daddy!"

"Hey, little man, are you okay?" He bent down and gave Steven a big hug. Steven started to cry out, "Mommy! Mommy!"

"I know, I know, you are safe, Steven, I got you." Joe thanked Cathy for everything and for not wanting to press charges against Elaine. "It's okay, Joe, there is something wrong with her, but I know that was not really her. She's really sweet and kind, but that was not Elaine; that was someone else."

"Yeah, from what you told me, that was not Elaine at all, but I should have known; she was not acting right this morning." Joe didn't mean for that to slip out; he was afraid Cathy was going to question him about it, but nothing came up. Cathy just gave Joe a hug and said, "You should take Steven home and make sure he gets some rest." Joe took her advice and took Steven home and laid Steven on the couch so he could sleep. As soon as Steven hit the couch, he was out like a light.

After a couple of hours of restless sleep, Steven woke up. He looked around and thought it was all a nightmare. He realized it wasn't. He saw the stack of black trash bags in the middle of the living room and he saw that his room was a mess when he looked over from the couch. Steven got up and rubbed his eyes. He could hear his dad's voice coming from the kitchen. Steven walked slowly and overheard his father talking on the phone. "Yeah, I'm not lying. No, I don't know how long she will be in the hospital, but I can't keep having Steven stay over at the neighbors. I feel guilty about it, plus I want family to watch him so he can have a feeling of a semi-normal home. Yeah, that would be great, I can pick you up next Sunday at the airport, try to get an evening flight. Okay, thanks again, I really appreciate it. I love you, Mom, see you next week."

EPISODE TWO

About three years had passed since Elaine's episode. Steven's grandmother, Jasmine, flew in from New York City a week after Elaine was admitted into the state mental hospital. Jasmine took care of Steven for about two years, giving him nurturing love and lots of home-cooked meals. Steven loved his grandma dearly. Jasmine was fairly old, she had Joe when she was in her mid-thirties—the same as Elaine and Joe when they had Steven together. Jasmine's old age did not slow her down; she may be seventy, but she is a firecracker. She acts young for her age and can keep up with about anyone half her age.

While Elaine was sick, drifting in and out of hospitals, rehabilitation homes, and sometimes placed in halfway homes before she could go back in general public, Jasmine acted as a mother to Steven. He was sad when she had to leave six months ago when Elaine finally recovered and was well enough to come home. Joe was very appreciative of his mother for watching Steven, not just to help provide a relatively stable home, but also keeping child protective services out of the picture.

Topeka is the capital city of Kansas, with a population of about 120,000. But it is still small enough that word gets around quickly. When Elaine had her major episode, it didn't take long for CPS to come knocking on Joe's door. Luckily for him, they arrived after Jasmine had flown down from New York. Jasmine and Joe convinced CPS that Jasmine was living with them, which was partly true. Jasmine's intention was to stay as long as it took for Elaine to get better, which eventually took nearly two and a half years. Jasmine stayed for about an additional three months after Elaine came home to make sure she was fit enough to take care of Steven herself.

What most people don't realize is that Elaine is a great mother. She is very caring, loving, and is a really great cook. It's when Elaine has an episode, or leading up to it, she changes completely. Jasmine realized how well Elaine was doing, so she decided to leave after feeling comfortable enough to do so. Steven missed his grandmother dearly and was still uneasy around his mother; he still loved her, but he had horrible nightmares from the events of three years ago. Often, the nightmares would continue for days, but then they would not happen for weeks. When they came, Steven had a hard time getting good sleep. In the end, it was all the same, he was scared to ever see his mother like that again.

On a cool, early, October evening. Steven was watching TV with his mother and father. They were watching Steven's favorite show at the time, *The Dukes of Hazard*. Steven loved watching the "General Lee" drive around the country, side jumping over ramps, getting away from the bad guys, going fast. He would always tell his parents "one of these days, I'm going to have a Dodge Charger! I'm going to drive it all around town and show it off to everyone!" he would always say excitedly while taking his toy General Lee and making "vroom, vroom" noises while running around the living room.

"Well, when you get older and get a job, you can save up for your own Charger," Joe said smiling while taking a sip of beer.

"Steven, just make sure you don't drive fast like they do in the TV show—don't forget, it's just a show."

"I know, Mom," Steven said, sounding deflated. Then the General Lee's horn went off and Steven glued himself back to the TV, happy as if there was not a care in the world.

As the episode was about to end, there was a knock at the front door. "Who could that be? It must be close to nine p.m.," Joe said while setting his beer on the coffee table and getting up to answer the door. Steven got up and walked behind his father to see who it was. Joe opened the front door and there were two police officers standing on the porch. Joe flicked on the porch light to help see better, and after a little bit of looking at the two officers, it hit him; it was the same two officers who had tackled Elaine and taken her off when she had her episode a few years back.

"Hello, may I help you?" Joe asked, his heart racing a little. He had consumed several beers tonight, not enough to be drunk, but enough to be tipsy, and after the whole CPS ordeal when Jasmine was over, he was worried. The officer's black uniforms blended in with the darkness behind them. "Hello, is Elaine Frankie McMurphy home tonight?" asked officer Tony

Smith. He was a little shorter than his partner, Pat Holmes, but they were yin and yang to each other. Tony was smaller but highly educated in law, and Pat was larger and more athletic, so they always worked well together on the beat.

"Yeah, she is, is there something wrong?"

"Well, yes, but we cannot tell you, we have to speak with Elaine. Don't worry, no one is in trouble, it's just we have some news to give to Elaine about a family member."

"Okay, I'll go get her real quick." Joe walked over to the couch and told Elaine what was going on. Steven still hid behind his father, Steven was young when he met these cops, but he remembered every detail of that day. His dreams reminded him of everything that happened that day and of everyone who was involved.

Elaine came slowly to the door and saw the two officers. They remembered her, but she did not remember them. Officer Smith cleared his throat.

"Elaine Frankie McMurphy?"

"Yes, I am Elaine, may I help you?" she asked, with a questioning eye.

"Well, we are here to inform you about your older brother Terry."

"Terry? I just spoke to him last week, is there something wrong with him?" Elaine had worry in her voice, and the expression on her face darkened. She knew there was something wrong; it's not every night two officers come to give you news about a loved one.

Officer Smith stared at Elaine for a few seconds and cleared his throat again. "Elaine, I'm sorry to inform you but your brother died earlier tonight."

"Died?" Elaine said, tears swelling up in her eyes. "What happened, was he murdered?"

"No, he committed suicide, and you are next of kin, so we wanted to inform you in person. We are very sorry for your loss."

Elaine began to cry; she was very close to her brother. Even though he lived in Tulsa, OK, they still talked a lot on the phone and she would write letters to him on special occasions. They had been through a lot growing up and he understood her illness. Joe tried to understand, but Terry grew up with her and knew her better than anyone else. After gaining her composure, Elaine wiped her eyes and looked at the two officers. "May I ask how he died?" She was afraid to hear how. Officer Smith looked at Holmes and then back at Elaine.

"Are you sure?"

"Why do you ask that, of course I do."

"Well, it's because it is fairly graphic and, . . ." Elaine cut Officer Smith off.

"Yes, I want to know how my older brother died. It will eat me up. I'll be kept up at night running different scenarios in my head. At least, if I know the exact how, I don't have to make up the way he died." The sound of desperation and sadness echoed in the night. Then officer Smith told Elaine how Terry died:

"Tulsa police were called in by a citizen who was driving down Highway 75. The caller said they saw a body hanging from a tree, but it was dark outside, and the caller didn't want to get too close to the body. When the police arrived, they saw

Terry's body hanging from a tree, but that wasn't all. There was a gunshot wound to the temple and a pistol laying on the ground below him. Apparently, from what we can make out, he hung himself but did not die from the hanging itself, so he must have brought a pistol for that reason, in case the hanging didn't do the job. Since he didn't die from the initial hanging, he shot himself to finish off the job, and that is how the Tulsa police found him, hanging with a . . ."

"Okay, you don't have to tell me anymore." Elaine said closing her eyes, leaning against the doorway. She began to cry softly, then her mourning began to grow louder. Steven came up from his dad.

"Mom, what's wrong, are you okay?"

"Oh, Terry, why, why couldn't of you told me you were suffering!"

"Uncle Terry?" Steven's eyes grew wide. Steven had met Terry only once. It was when his mom was in the hospital. He visited Elaine not too long before his Grandma, Jasmine, left. Steven loved Uncle Terry. When Terry came, he gave Steven a handmade baseball bat, with his name engraved in the handle. Steven enjoyed watching baseball and was wanting to try out for little league next year. Terry was a great wood worker and knew how much Steven loved baseball; he also gave Steven a nice baseball glove and some new cleats. Steven may have only met Terry in person once, but he talked to him on the phone monthly even before he met his uncle in person, and now Steven was concerned.

"Mom, what happened to Uncle Terry?" Elaine turned her head and went to Steven; she knelt down, hugged him, and began to cry while saying, "Uncle Terry is dead, Steven." Steven then began to slowly cry. Joe was silent, he walked to the kitchen to make a drink. The officers knew their time were done and silently left the front porch while Steven and Elaine cried through the dark, moonless night.

Two weeks had passed since Terry's death. Steven was affected deeply by the loss. Steven would hold the bat his uncle made him each night and tear up. Not only did his uncle give him this bat, it was something he made with his own hands, Steven never had anything made just for him. He remembered all the conversations he had with his uncle and his Uncle's funny sense of humor. When Steven was down or picked on at school, his Uncle always knew how to perk him up.

Elaine, on the other hand, was severely affected by the loss of her older brother. She began to grow depressed and started to sleep longer and longer each day. It got to the point Elaine would just lay in bed all day, only to emerge to eat and go to the bathroom. Joe was getting worried, because he remembered what happened the last time Elaine laid around all day. Joe figured this had to be different because her brother died, and Joe could sympathize, because he lost his own father when he was only fourteen. Joe remembered how affected he was by it.

It was a sunny and warm Monday morning, in October. Steven got up out of bed to get ready for school. When he got to the living room, he saw his mother in the kitchen, which was a new sight for him.

"Mom, are you making breakfast?"

"Yes, honey, I'm making bacon, eggs, and pancakes." The smell of pancakes hit Steven, he loved pancakes more than anything else for breakfast.

"Oh, wow, thanks!"

"You're welcome, now go sit down and I'll bring them to you." Joe walked into the kitchen after taking a shower; he was surprised to see Elaine up and cooking this morning. He wanted to ask her if she was feeling better, but he was afraid it would bring up bad memories for Elaine, plus he didn't want to ruin the moment.

"Oh, wow, you're making breakfast this morning, it smells great."

"You want anything before you go to work?" Elaine said, with a big smile on her face, beaming as bright as the sun filtering through the windows.

"Oh, no, I'm okay, I have to go into work early today, I was just coming to let you know that I'm leaving."

"Oh, okay." Then Elaine put a plate in front of Steven.

"I'll see you guys after work. Steven, you have a good day at school."

"Okay, Dad."

Steven began to stuff his mouth with pancakes drenched with maple syrup. As Joe was leaving, he had a weird feeling, Elaine seemed way too happy this morning, but he shrugged it off, he figured that Elaine may have finally come to terms with Terry's death and maybe cooking and moving around was helping to clear her mind. Joe got into his pickup and headed off for work.

"Okay, Steven, you should go take a shower before school."

"Okay," said Steven, even though he was seven, he loved to take showers, something about the warm water hitting his body made him feel better than taking a bath. He stopped taking baths when he was six last year. His grandma was surprised at how much a six-year-old loved showers. Most kids hated to even take baths at his age, but he always loved a nice, long, warm shower in the morning.

Steven got into the shower and started playing with some of his toys. He loved to put some rags into the drain to raise up six inches of water, so he could play with his toy boats. Stomping around making the boats bob up and down made him laugh. He felt like he was in control of the situation—something he himself could control. After a while, the water would get cold and Steven would let the water drain, then he would quickly get to the actual cleaning part of the shower. This was his usual routine, playing first, then he would wash himself at the very end when the water began to get cold. Steven scrubbed himself down and turned off the water. He got out of the shower and realized he had taken nearly thirty minutes; he was going to be late to school, if he didn't hurry up. Quickly, he dried off, brushed his teeth, fixed his light brown hair, and put on his clothes. As he was stepping out, he heard dishes banging around in the kitchen. He stepped out of the bathroom and walked into the living room to a large pile of black, trash bags.

Steven stared at the pile of trash bags and then he heard a loud crash from the kitchen.

"Mom . . . are you okay?" he ran to the kitchen.

"Yes, honey, I just dropped some dishes on the floor, can

you help me clean it up?"

Steven hesitated; he was wanting to know why there was a pile of filled, black, trash bags in the middle of the living room.

"I'll grab the broom and dustpan."

As Steven was cleaning up the mess, he saw his mom starting to empty all of the cupboards and placing all the dishes in black bags. Then she would walk to the living room and place them on the pile. Steven had to know why.

"Mom, what are you doing?"

"I'm cleaning, silly, what does it look like?" Elaine walked into Steven's room and came out with his clothes, bedding, and toys, then she began packing them into trash bags. Steven remembered the last time he saw this kind of pile and it brought back memories—memories that were previously replaced by the loss of his uncle.

"Mom, are you okay?"

"Yes, honey, I'm okay, I had to clean the house."

"But why, Mom, the house looked fine earlier, I kept up on my chores like you and dad asked."

"I know Steven, but I was told to clean the house, Terry wants the house clean for his stay."

"Terry? But Uncle Terry is dead mom." Steven began to feel uncomfortable.

"No, he's not; he's standing right behind you—he's the one that helped get half of these bags into the living room. Now go on to school, you'll be late."

Steven looked around; it was only him and his mom. He knew Uncle Terry was dead, but his mom said he's in the room with them.

"Mom, Terry isn't here."

"Yes, he is—he's right behind you, he wants the house clean while he . . ."

"Yes, I know, you just said that"

Steven felt strange about the whole situation, his dad had already left for work and Steven didn't know what to do. He had to get to school; maybe his mom just missed her brother so much that she really thought he was there. Steven decided to leave for school. "Bye, Mom, I'll see you after school." As he was closing the door, he faintly heard his mom saying, "Okay, Terry and I will be here." Then Steven walked across the street to meet up with Zack and Katy.

Steven walked across the street and joined Zack and Katy at their front porch. "Hey, Steven, you're running late, we were about to leave without you."

"I know, I'm sorry, just some stuff happening, that is all." They started to head towards school. Lundgren Elementary was not a far walk, only about four blocks down the road and one block over to the east, so it would only take them about fifteen minutes to get there. They would make it on time, as long as Zack and Steven didn't get distracted kicking rocks or throwing them at each other.

A cool breeze blew across Steven and it made him shiver; it was still fairly warm for late October, but he did not like the cold at all and the breeze made him shiver down to his core. However, he did enjoy the colors of fall while walking and it was a welcoming site to him. The sun was out and filtered through the red, orange, and yellow leaves and despite what Steven was thinking about earlier, it was nice to see the beauty of fall. After looking at the leaves, he knew that soon the cold would come, win over fall and the leaves would sprinkle the earth.

They were about halfway to school when Zack broke the silence, "You doing okay, Steven? You haven't said anything the whole time or wanted to play along the way," Zack asked, picking up a rock in his hand. Katy nudged Zack on the arm to drop it and whispered, "Hey, I don't think Steven is up for playing this morning." Then she pointed to Steven. He was looking down, he looked downcast and sad. Zack knew that Steven's uncle had passed away a couple of weeks ago and thought that maybe Steven was just having some deep thoughts about his uncle at this moment. "Yeah," Zack whispered back, "I guess I shouldn't play with him, I just thought it might perk him up, but the way he looks, it may just make him mad instead. I'll see how he is during recess; he may want to play then." Zack didn't say another word, until all three reached the school.

They made it to class on time and Zack separated from Katy and Steven. Zack was three grades ahead of them and was in the fifth grade, Katy and Steven had the same second grade teacher, Ms. Williams, so they walked to class together while Zack went to another class. Then Zack grabbed Katy and pulled her to the side

"Hey, watch over Steven, okay?"

"Okay, Zack, I will." And Zack went to class.

Ms. Williams was writing down the day's lesson on the blackboard when Katy and Steven walked in. She was a young teacher, late twenties, with long, flowing, blond hair, deep hazel eyes and always wore suit pants, with a business casual top. She was really nice to her kids and they all loved her, but she also had a temper when the kids acted bad. She was both admired and respected. "Hello, Steven and Katy, you guys almost made it late . . ." and the bell rang right when Steven and Katy sat down in their seats. "Well, I guess you guys were saved by the bell, so you were right on time, so no tardy slips today." She winked and turned back around to writing out the first lesson of the day.

Steven was a quiet kid in class. He would participate only when he absolutely knew the correct answer. He was always afraid to try to answer questions he might not know, so he wouldn't look dumb. He didn't want another thing to be picked on about. The first half of the day went without trouble. Steven hoped today would go smoothly so he could go home and see if his mom was okay. He was hoping that spectacle this morning was just a fluke and that maybe his mom was just so down about Uncle Terry that this was a weird way of coping. He didn't really know; he was only seven and didn't know how all adults acted. He thought his mom was normal, until he got picked on for having the "weird mom" which the kids would always say to him, plus point, laugh and throw rocks. He liked to play throwing stones with Zack, but they would throw to catch, not to hurt, but the other kids would throw big rocks at Steven, sometimes at his head, sometimes at his lower waist. He hated it when kids would pick on him, that is why he was quiet most of the time. Yet, if he was too quiet, he would be picked on for being the quiet kid, so he would answer questions Ms. William would often times ask the class. But again, he would only answer the ones he absolutely knew.

Before Steven knew it, the bell for lunch sounded. He got up, got in line as usual and headed towards the cafeteria. He sat down with Katy and ate quietly. "Steven, you have not said anything this morning, or during class." Steven stayed silent, quietly eating. "Are you okay?" she scooted closer to him. Steven liked Katy, she was a little, pudgy girl, but always had a smile like her mom. The sun from the cafeteria windows hit her light brown eyes and curly, brown hair and it made her glow. Steven always thought she was cute, but he liked her more as a sister, just as he viewed Zack as an older brother. Steven replied:

"Yeah, I'm okay, just thinking."

"Oh, so you are alive," she lightly jabbed Steven in the arm, he didn't say anything.

"Hey, I'm just kidding."

"I know, I just want to be left alone today, I'm sorry." Then Steven went back to eating. Katy didn't want to push her luck; she at least got a response. She went back to talking to her other friends at the table.

Recess always came after lunch. Most of the time, Steven liked recess; it was when he would play with Zack. Zack protected Steven as a little brother and usually people would leave Steven alone when he was with Zack. Zack was big for his age; he wasn't just big as in husky, but he was pretty athletic and under all the weight was a good amount of muscle. He was also pretty tall, and most kids wouldn't ever dream of fighting Zack. Lucky for them, Zack wasn't a bully, he usually protected the kids who got bullied. But when Zack was home sick or doing some extra credit for classes he was behind on—that is when the kids picked on Steven. Sadly, today was a day that Zack had to stay inside during recess to make up some credits for reading; he scored low on a words per minute reading test and had to be tutored today. Steven did not like the idea that Zack had to stay inside while he was outside. So, he did what he felt would keep himself from everyone and walked to the big tree in the middle of the school yard, sat under it and began to read, hoping no one would disturb him.

As Steven was reading, he realized recess was halfway over. He was starting to relax when someone came up to him and took the book out of his hand and threw it to the side. The book skidded across the blacktop making a scratching noise. "Hey, Steven, where's your bodyguard today?" Steven looked up and saw it was Tanner Downs. Tanner was the second biggest kid after Zack, but Tanner liked to pick on Steven the most, ever since word got around about Steven's mom running around naked several years back. Tanner loved to pick on Steven about it.

"Heard your uncle died, I'm sorry to hear that." Steven looked up surprised, was Tanner really sympathizing with him? "Just kidding" then Tanner pushed Steven to the ground on his back. "What are you going to do? We all know you never fight back. Your dad's an alcoholic and your mom is a weirdo." Then Tanner began to laugh, his yellow teeth and bleach blonde hair reflecting off the noon sun.

"My dad is not an alco . . . alco . . ." Steven didn't really know what an alcoholic was, but he knew it was not a nice thing to say about his dad. "Alcoholic, he likes to drink beer a lot" and Tanner looked over to the other older kids and began laughing.

"This moron doesn't even know how to say alcoholic. Well, I know you can say weird, as in your mom is a big weirdo." And Tanner started to laugh more.

Steven was starting to tear up. "Oh, is the little boy with the weird mom going to cry?" Tanner began to laugh even more. "Hey, everyone, look at the little, cry baby, with the weird mom—remember? She's the one who ran around town naked!" Steven was tearing up even more, then before he realized it, he uttered, "My mom isn't weird." Tanner stopped laughing. "What was that, cry baby? You say something?" Tanner started to get closer to Steven; Tanner's face was growing red. "Hey, I was talking to you, you say something smart to me?"

Steven stared down at the ground; he was starting to get angry. The years of torment from Tanner, and the loss of his uncle and his mom acting weird this morning were stressful. Steven knew his mom was different, but he was seven and didn't like it when other kids made fun of him about his mom. Suddenly, Steven yelled out and jumped towards Tanner. "My mom is not weird." Tanner laughed and stepped aside. "Big mistake, little, cry baby," Tanner said and started taunting while pointing at Steven. "Your mom is a weirdo," he said over and over, then he pushed Steven down and was about to start punching him when his fist was held back.

"You leave Steven alone, Tanner, or I'll kick your ass." It was

Zack, Tanner turned around and froze.

"Oh my, Zack, I was just playing with Steven . . . I thought you were inside."

"I was, but I saw what was going on. By the way, you are the moron, the window is only twenty feet from the tree, and I heard everything." Then Zack twisted Tanner around and threw him to the ground. "If you mess with Steven again, I'll come over to your house and kick your ass personally. Now say sorry to Steven." Tanner just stared at Zack, then Steven, then to the gathering crowd. "Hurry up before the teachers come, Ms. Williams knew I was coming to stop this fight peacefully and if there is anything more, we will all be in trouble. Now say sorry to Steven and leave," Zack said while helping Steven get up. "Sorry, Steven," Tanner muttered just enough for Zack to hear.

"You should say it like you mean it, Tanner."

"No, at least I said it." Then Tanner walked off and whispered so no one could hear, "His mom is a freaking weirdo though." Then the end of recess bell rang, and the kids went back to class for the rest of the day.

After school, Steven, Zack, and Katy were walking home. Steven kept to himself and noticed that despite the sun still being out, it was dropping in temperature and he was beginning to feel cold. Besides the situation with Tanner during recess, luckily for Steven, the rest of the school day was uneventful. Zack was walking ahead, so he slowed his pace to get next to Steven.

"Hey, I know you are not in the mood to talk, but I have to talk to you." Steven kept quiet. Zack didn't grow mad or irritated, he just kept on talking. "Okay, well at least listen. I think that maybe we should start working on you standing up for yourself." Steven looked at Zack. "Okay, good, so I do have your attention. What I am saying is that I'm in the fifth grade and next year I'm going to middle school; I won't be around to protect you."

Realization hit Steven; he had thought about it, but with his uncle's death and the constant dreams about his mother, he took advantage of the now. "Well, I think that maybe we should start learning how you can protect yourself, or at least to keep the situation from getting worse." Steven looked at Zack and was wanting to say something but realized they were almost home.

"Maybe you should come over now and we can start."

"I can't"

"Why? Usually, your parents don't care if you come over after school."

The truth was that Steven wanted to go straight home; he wanted to see how his mom was doing. He had been thinking about it all day. Yes, his uncle's death still affected him, but what he witnessed this morning just kept eating at him. He started to relive what happened three years ago. He may have only been four at the time, but the inner conscious always remembers, especially when that conscious is your dreams that are constantly reminding you of that day.

Zack looked at Steven; the way he said "I can't" sounded different, like Steven wanted too, but can't, so he left it alone. "Well, if you decide to come by later, I'll be home, if not, maybe we can start tomorrow, sounds okay?" Steven just blankly said "yes" and went back to being silent the last block of the way home. Soon they all got to the curb of Zack's and Katy's home. "I'll see you later, Steven," Katy said, then she ran up the walkway and went into the house. Zack stood there looking at Steven as he headed towards his house. He viewed Steven as a little brother and cared for him; he knew Steven had a different family life than others, but Zack didn't care, Steven himself was a great friend and that's what mattered to him, then Zack walked up the porch and went inside.

Steven walked up to his front door and tried opening it; the door was locked. He thought it was weird that it was locked, since his mom was home or was supposed to be home. He knocked on the door and no one answered. He looked under the porch to find the rock where they kept an emergency key just in case, but it was gone. Steven began to grow scared; he was afraid someone might have come and done something to his mom. He started pounding on the door, just to make sure, but no one answered. Then he walked to the window to see inside the house, luckily the blinds were halfway opened— enough so that he could see inside. What he saw made him grow cold. He saw the same pile of black trash bags from this morning, but larger, much larger. Not only that, all the furniture in the house was piled up in the center of the room along with the trash bags. "What the . . ." Then his mom popped up in front of the window and stared right at Steven; it startled him so much he jumped and fell back. He got up then walked to the door.

"Mom, let me in, it's Steven, I just saw you." Then he heard a yell come from inside the house but could not make out what she was saying. He went back to the window but saw that his mom was gone. His heart began to race and he decided he was going to go next door, so he could have Cathy call his dad and let him know his mom had locked him out. But right when he turned around to leave, he heard the door swing open and before he could react, he was pulled into the house, a hand gripped across his mouth.

Steven was dragged into the house and thrown onto the pile of trash bags. "What do you want with me and Terry?" Steven stared at his mother, speechless; he only saw his mom.

"Answer me, what do you want with us? You can't have him, he's my brother."

"Mom, it's me, Steven." He said panicky.

"Steven?"

"Yes, Mom, Ste . . ."

"Why do you keep calling me mom, I am not your mother, I could never be a mother to a demon." The word demon hit Steven to the core. He remembered when his mother attacked Cathy, she kept calling her a demon.

"Mo . . ."

"I said don't call me mom!"

Then Elaine came towards Steven, but Steven rolled over off the trash bags and headed towards the door. Luckily, Elaine forgot to lock the door, so he was able to open it quickly. Elaine turned back around and went chasing after Steven. Quickly, Steven shut the door and kept holding onto the handle. He was only seven, but pure adrenaline gave him great strength for a boy his age. His size was no match for his mother, who had tremendous strength when she was like this. Elaine pulled the door open. "You can't have my brother, Terry is mine." Steven fell when the door was pulled open. Elaine fell back and landed on the trash bags. Steven got back up and ran and didn't look back; he ran straight towards Cathy's, looked back and saw that his mom was gone. She went back in the house. He was relieved, he thought his mom would follow him, but she seemed more worried about Terry, even though Terry was not there, Steven realized that his mother was just fending him off . . . but she attacked him and tears began to swell in his eyes. He knocked on the door of Cathy's house. A second later she answered. "Hello, Steven, what's wrong?" Steven began to cry and told Cathy everything that had just happened. Cathy immediately called Joe and he came home as soon as he learned what had happened.

When Joe got home, he walked to the door and tried to open it, but it was locked.

"Elaine, let me in." Elaine shouted from behind the door

"No, you can't have Terry, I won't lose him again."

"Elaine, Terry is dead."

Then the door opened, and Elaine was staring straight at Joe. Joe was a little taller than Elaine and he was heavier; his brown eyes grew wide. This was the first time he had seen Elaine like this. The last time, he caught the tail end of it when she was being hauled off by the police.

"He is not dead; he is right behind me." Elaine screamed at Joe, her face was red with anger, and her eyes blazed with such ferocity that Joe grew uneasy. "Elai . . ." but right before he could finish his sentence, Elaine ran past Joe and down the street. When Elaine rushed past Joe, he heard her say, "Come on, Terry, follow me."

Joe ran into the house and called the police. It didn't take long for the police to find Elaine. She was walking down the street a couple of blocks down yelling at passing cars, "He's mine, you can't take him." When the police approached her, she ran away yelling, "you can't have my brother." The police were aware that she was actually alone and that there was no Terry, also it was officers Tony Smith and Pat Holmes, the two officers who detained her three years ago and the same ones who informed her about her brother's death. Eventually, the officers got Elaine and she was sent to the State Mental Hospital after she was evaluated at the local hospital in town. They transferred her to the mental hospital, since it was better equipped for this situation.

Later that night, Steven heard his father talking to his grandmother. He was reliving the same moment, his father telling her everything, asking her to come and etc. Steven didn't care; all he could think about was Tanner. What he said about his mother kept ringing in his ears. "Your mom is a weirdo" and Tanner's laugh echoed in his mind. He went back to his bed and began to cry. "My mom really is weird," he whispered to himself till he cried himself to sleep.

EPISODE THREE

Two years had passed, since Elaine's last major episode, following the death of her brother, Terry. Steven, who was almost ten, had become more and more removed from both home life and from his best friend, Zack. Once Steven returned home from school, he immediately went to his bedroom to play on his Nintendo 64 that he got for Christmas. It is the only thing that can keep his mind off his mother's episodes that he horrifically witnessed for the past several years. Steven's grades have not suffered, and he maintains a fairly consistent average which is why Joe does not care that Steven plays video games all evening. As long as Steven makes decent grades and is caught up on all of his schoolwork, Joe does not care that Steven locks himself up in his room and says nothing to him or Jasmine.

Jasmine is again staying with Joe to watch Steven while Elaine is away. During the past two years, Elaine has been drifting in and out of mental hospitals. The doctors cannot seem to get her on a regimen that works for her. Elaine will come home seemingly better, but in a week or two, she starts showing signs of paranoia, agitation, depression and then she will hallucinate. Joe usually sends her to the hospital as soon as she exhibits signs, and then the cycle repeats itself. The last mini episode as Joe likes to call them, because they are not as severe as the two major ones she has had, was still enough to send her to the state mental hospital where she had been for the last three months. The doctors this time think they may have found the right combination of medications.

Jasmine has stayed with Joe and Steven for the past two years. Even though Elaine had been coming home during this span, Jasmine wanted to make sure Elaine was well enough to be trusted. During this time, Jasmine had been playing Elaine, both in an emotional way for Steven, and even physically by telling CPS over the phone that she was Elaine. CPS has yet to meet Elaine; every time CPS calls Steven's home, Jasmine is there to pick it up and play the part as Elaine. However, the next day would be different as Steven would soon find out.

"Thanks, Dad, for dropping me off at school," Steven said while grabbing his backpack from the back of the bed of his dad's Dodge. "No problem," Joe said while taking a swig from his jug that Steven knew was really whiskey and water mixed together.

"Now remember, when Mrs. Schmidt asks you where your mom is, what do you tell her?"

"She is at home."

"And if she does not pick up?" Joe said looking at Steven reassuringly.

"That if mom does not pick up, then she is probably out

getting groceries."

"Good," Joe said smiling. "What if she asks to come over to the house?"

"To tell her that mom works part time at Fur's Diner."

"And if she asks for mom's schedule?"

"To remind her that mom works swing shifts and picks up shifts when other workers call out and that her schedule is not a good reflection of when she is off?" Joe smiled and hugged Steven.

"Dad, what if Mrs. Schmidt asks if mom is picking up, why can't she come over that minute, she'll know that Grandma, or who she thinks is mom, is at home and go within the hour?"

"Well, if Grandma picks up, she'll know what to tell her." Joe said laughing.

"What if Mrs. Schmidt does not tell her she is coming and just goes?"

"Steven, Steven, do not worry about it, Grandma knows what to do, just leave it in her hands."

"Okay, Dad, whatever you say. I'll see you tonight when you get off work." Then Steven hopped out of the truck and headed to class. Joe watched as Steven walked into school and drove off.

It was a chilly start to spring. The first week of April, in Topeka, KS, can either be cold and rainy, or nice and warm, with plenty of sunshine to welcome blooming flowers and to give color. However, this week was one of those cold and rainy starts. Steven looked outside and saw that the trees have yet to bloom and that the grass was still brown and padded down from the hard, previous winter. Steven's mood usually reflected the weather and since his mom was in the hospital again, he felt even lower.

Before Steven realized it, the lunch bell rung. Today was Tuesday, and his anxiety was high. Most kids were excited when it was lunch time, but not Steven. Every Tuesday, Mrs. Schmidt would pull him from lunch so he could eat with her in her room while asking him questions about his home life. He always answered the same questions the exact same way his father told him to. Steven didn't hate Mrs. Schmidt, he just knew his mom was different and that Mrs. Schmidt wanted to know more about her and it made Steven uncomfortable talking about his mom, especially when it was his Grandmother Jasmine who was really the one talking to Mrs. Schmidt on the phone.

Steven walked into the gym where the lunch tables were set up; he really wanted to sit alone and eat his lunch. He just wanted to go home, lock himself up in his room and play video games, until he had to go to bed. The gym was lit solely by the overhead lights. Usually, when the sun was out, it would filter through the big windows that surrounded the top half of the gymnasium. It was a welcoming and calming feeling for Steven when the sun was out and filtering its glorious rays into the gym. It made him feel warm . . . and happy, which is something he did not feel very often. The clouds gave way to darkness and a downpour was drenching the windows of the gym. Every now and again, sounds of thunder would rattle the windows and it made Steven grow uncomfortable.

Soon, Steven went through the lunch line and grabbed his food. Today was chicken nuggets and mashed potatoes. Steven really did not care much for the food; he just knew he had to eat. For him, food was just sustenance and he really did not care what it was, just as long as it was edible. After he got his food, he knew it was pointless to try to find a spot to sit, because Mrs. Schmidt would be at her usual spot by the front doors waiting for him. He looked towards the door and saw her standing there with her arms folded and a smile on her face. She then saw Steven and waved him over to her.

Mrs. Schmidt was a nice woman. She was a little overweight but was fairly young. Her black, curly hair was always done in the same perm for the year and a half that Steven had known her. She wore thick, black-framed glasses that were round. Steven has seen pictures of John Lennon before, because his dad loved the Beatles; so, whenever he saw Mrs. Schmidt, he always thought of Lennon's glasses, but thicker and uglier. Steven did like Mrs. Schmidt's personality. She always talked in a calm manner and seemed to be very easy going which was calming to Steven.

Steven walked over to her. "Hello, Steven, how are you today?" She said extending an arm out to him to get a hug. "Fine," Steven said looking down and held his tray in one hand while giving a non-caring half hug to Mrs. Schmidt. "Great, follow me." Mrs. Schmidt turned around and walked, with Steven trailing behind her. Steven really did not know why she kept coming to get him, he could go there himself, he knew exactly where her room was, what time he needed to be there and what days.

"Okay, Steven, please have a seat." Mrs. Schmidt walked over to her chair extending her arm to the chair that Steven always sat in. Steven placed his tray on her old, oak desk that seemed to have been there when the school first opened in the late 1940s. He took a seat in the big, yellow, upholstered chair that sat directly in front of Mrs. Schmidt's desk. She sat in a red leather, office chair that was fairly worn. She always said how much she loved it, because it was the first nice thing she bought when she graduated from college and wanted to celebrate her new job, by getting a brand-new leather office chair she had custom made.

Steven was hit by the usual patchouli candle that she always burned in her office. As he was eating his lunch, he looked around the room to see that it was still the same. The "Hang in there" picture with the cat was on the wall behind her, for some reason he always hated that poster. Then there was that "READ!" poster by her big shelf of books, half of them Steven could not pronounce. There was not much to her room. Steven always thought her room was misplaced. It was located behind the gym next to the utilities closet. It was a small room with only enough room for her desk, two chairs, and her bookshelf. Soon, Mrs. Schmidt broke the silence, after Steven was done eating.

"Okay, Steven, since you are done eating, let's talk about how you are doing." She said with a smile on her face and grabbing a notebook and pen from her drawer.

"Fine as usual"

"That is good," she said while looking down and writing down what Steven assumed was his word for word statement.

"How is your mom?"

"She is fine."

"Where is she at right now?"

"She is at home probably cleaning house as usual."

"If I should call her, would she answer the phone?"

"Yes, and if she did not, she is probably out shopping for groceries." Steven was getting bored. It was the same questions as always; he gave the usual responses. He knew that next she would go call his mom, or what she didn't know, his grandma, have a conversation, ask if she could come visit, and usually hang up sighing and saying to herself, "Well maybe next time." Steven was looking at the phone at her desk waiting for her to pick it up, but he was thrown off by a question he was never asked before.

"How is your dad, Steven?" Steven was never asked about his dad; his mom was always the topic of discussion. Steven felt everyone in the state of Kansas knew how his mom was and the things that have happened.

"Uh, he is fine, I guess." Steven looked down.

"What do you mean you guess?" Mrs. Schmidt said still looking down at her notepad while writing.

"He is doing fine."

"Does your dad work?"

"Yeah."

"Where at?"

"At Shooter's Sports Bar."

"Doing what?"

"He is the kitchen manager."

"I see."

Steven was getting worried. The last he knew, she thought he was still working at the steak house, because that is what his dad told people, except that in reality his dad had not worked there in four years. His dad had job-hopped the last four years from restaurant to restaurant. He did not know why his dad had six different jobs in the last four years, but his dad always told him, "Well, this one didn't work out."

"So, he works at a bar?" She said lifting her head to look at him.

"Yeah"

"What does your dad do when he gets home from work?" Steven was getting restless; he didn't want to tell her the truth. His dad would come home late, eat some dinner and then drink several cans of beer, before passing out on the couch.

"He comes home and eats dinner with me and mom." Steven uttered, after a few moments of silence. Steven could hear Mrs. Schmidt lightly say "hmm" while writing in her notepad.

"What else does he do?" She asked after finishing her last sentence.

"He then watches the news or sports and then goes to bed."

"Does he play with you?" she asked, holding her pen in her hand. Steven and his dad had never played much together. Once in a while, his dad and he would play catch, for maybe ten minutes on a lucky day when his dad came home early from work. If it was his dad's day off, well, they never played on those days. Steven didn't want to tell her that in reality Steven just plays video games all evening and that his dad would come home, drink, then go to sleep.

"Yeah, we play catch."

"You didn't mention that earlier. You said he comes home

and eats with you before watching TV."

"Well, I forgot to mention that we play catch while mom is cooking dinner."

"Oh, so she does not cook before he comes home?"

"No," Steven said beginning to panic. His dad had never prepared him for this; he always rehearsed about his mom, never about his dad. He was beginning to worry that she may be catching on to his lies about his dad. Did someone mention to the school about his dad's drinking? "She cooks when he gets home so it gives us time to play or Dad to talk to me about school."

"He talks to you about school?"

"Yeah, to see how my grades are." This was not an entire lie, his dad would ask him, but in the mornings when he was dropping Steven off to school.

"Okay, I see." Mrs. Schmidt then began to write into her notepad more and, with every movement of the pen, Steven grew more and more restless. He wanted this interview to end. He just wanted to go home and be alone in his bedroom. "One last thing, Steven." She said while closing her notepad.

"Yeah," Steven said, looking at the closed notepad.

"Do you know what alcohol is?" She asked while pushing her glasses back up her nose that probably slid down while her head was down while writing.

"Yeah," Steven said, looking down.

"Good, tell me what you think it is."

"I guess it's stuff like beer."

"Okay, what else?" Steven did not want to tell her he was aware of other things like whiskey, rum, vodka, and gin, but he just told her "just beer really, I just know beer is not good for you."

"Why is that?" she said looking harder at Steven.

"Because my dad always tells me to never drink beer."

"Does your dad drink beer, Steven?" Steven knew beer was bad, so he told her, "No, he does not drink it."

"Are you sure Steven?"

"Yeah."

"Do you know what a beer can looks like or the different brands?"

"Yes, I can read you know." Steven did not mean to sound snarky, but he did not want to tell her the truth that his dad drinks mainly beer.

"What does your dad drink then?"

"He drinks water and . . . and . . . Coke!" he said quickly. He had to think of something quick and Coke cans are red, just like the Budweiser cans his dad actually drinks.

"I see" Mrs. Schmidt said to herself and then opened the notepad back open and wrote some more things down. Steven tried to see what she was writing but he saw she was writing in cursive and he could not read it upside down, it all just looked like continuous scribble to him.

"Okay, Steven, I am going to call your mom and see how she is doing." Steven felt a little better; he was glad the subject of his dad was done. He sat there and listened to the usual conversation and the rest of it went according to usual. She hung up, but instead of saying "Maybe next time" she walked over to the windows and saw that the rain has let up. She then walked over and grabbed her red trench coat and walked

Steven to the door. "Thank you, Steven. I will see you next week." Steven was wondering where she was going.

"Are you leaving early today, Mrs. Schmidt?"

"No, I just have a meeting to go to." She said smiling at Steven and then she walked him to his class. Steven sat in class worried, he was wondering where Mrs. Schmidt was really going. Something deep down inside him told him that she was going to do a surprise visit to his house and realize his grandma was really his mom.

Mrs. Schmidt arrived at Steven's house around two in the afternoon. The rain had stopped and the clouds were beginning to thin enough, so that the sky turned a bright white from the sun hiding behind the clouds. The light blue house had one car in front of it, it was a yellow, 1976 Dodge Aspen. She looked into her notes and double checked that Joe drove a Dodge pickup truck so she hoped that Elaine drove the Aspen. She got out of her car and walked up to the small, blue, two-bedroom home. It was a quant home of nine hundred square feet, with two bedrooms, a living room, kitchen and one bathroom. She saw that there was a swing on the brown-painted, wooden porch and a gas grill at one end. She knocked on the door and soon heard someone approaching the door.

Elaine opened the door as if she was expecting her. Jasmine was standing behind Elaine and asking who it was.

"Hello, is Elaine McMurphy home?"

"Yes, I am Elaine, you must be Sarah Schmidt that I just spoke to on the phone. What a nice surprise; I did not know you would be coming over." Elaine motioned for Sarah to come into the house.

Elaine had just arrived from the State Mental Hospital and Jasmine filled her in on everything that was going on between herself and Sarah. Elaine seemed to understand what was going on and knew that Sarah probably worked with child protective services. Elaine has never been aware of her own episodes and thought that when she was in the hospital she was there for her depression. She always denied that she had episodes. She thought Sarah was there because of Joe's drinking problem and that someone may have talked to somebody at the school about the issue. What Elaine did not know was that Sarah was there because of issues with both Elaine and Joe.

Sarah walked over to Elaine and they talked for a bit while Jasmine stayed in the kitchen to prepare dinner.

"May I ask who she is, if you don't mind me asking?" Sarah said while finding a brown recliner and sitting in it.

"Her name is Jasmine; she is Steven's grandmother from New York."

"Oh, how nice, how long has she been here?" Sarah looked over at Jasmine to try to facilitate a hello from her; Jasmine just sat there quietly peeling some potatoes for tonight's roast dinner.

"Oh, she is just visiting for a couple of weeks; she usually comes about once a year to visit us."

"Oh, I see." Sarah looked again at Jasmine and said hello. Jasmine gave her a wave and went back to her work. Jasmine did not want to talk because she was afraid Sarah might recognize her voice. Sarah gave up and went back to Elaine.

"Your voice sounds different over the phone; you sound much younger."

"Yeah, people say that all the time, I don't know why but I have always been told my voice sounds fuller and deeper over the phone, but in person, it is a higher pitch." Elaine smiled at Sarah sitting across the small living room on the couch.

"Well, I am very happy to meet you in person, Elaine. It is always great to put a face to someone as everyone likes to say."

"Yes, the same can be said about you, too." Elaine kept her smile.

"May I ask you some questions, Elaine?"

"Go ahead." Sarah was really wanting to look around the house to find evidence of Joe's drinking problem. She felt unsure about Elaine. Elaine was very nice, but she just never seemed to be available. Today, however, with an unexpected visit she was home, but with another woman—Jasmine. Sarah suspected that perhaps Jasmine has been here longer, but she had no proof. So now she focused more on trying to pin the case down to Joe.

"What do you do for a living?" Sarah brought out her notepad and pen.

"Well, I worked part time at Fur's Diner as a waitress. It was more of an on-call basis. I only went in when too many people called off sick."

"Worked there?"

"Yes, I quit about a month ago, now I am a full-time stay-at-home mom." Sarah went to writing her notes. Steven made it sound like his mom still worked there.

"Okay, that sounds great to me. So, what does Joe do?"

"He is a kitchen manager at Shooter's Bar and Grille; he has been working there for about six months."

"What did he do before that?"

"He worked at a steakhouse for eight years but got burned out on it. He decided to try a different job that had different hours, or so he thought at the time—it ends up being about the same. But he seems to like this job more, because he comes home happier than with the last job."

"What do you mean by happier, was he angry?"

"No, nothing at that level, he just seemed more reclusive and self-absorbed. When Joe is unhappy, he does not talk much and keeps to himself a lot."

"I see." Sarah was furiously writing down her notes. She looked around and still could not see anything wrong. Everything was spotless in the living room. She decided to come up with a way to get into the kitchen and peek into the fridge. "May I have a drink, I am parched."

"Sure, what would you like?"

"A Coke if you have one."

"Okay, sounds good wait here."

"Is it okay if I come with you? I would like to talk more in the kitchen." Elaine didn't mind so she walked Sarah over to the kitchen. She opened the fridge and grabbed a Coke. Sarah could see in the fridge. She expected to see a bunch of beer cans in the fridge, but she saw nothing but food, milk, and pop. When they both got to the kitchen table, Jasmine headed to the bathroom.

Sarah looked around some more and did not see anything out of the ordinary. What she did not know was the fridge did have a twelve pack in it, but the crisper drawers in the fridge are white and that is where Joe put his beer. She also did not know that Joe did not keep a liquor cabinet; he kept all his hard liquor in a cabinet by the sink where many people would expect dishes. Jasmine made sure to keep the kitchen and house spotless and free of beer cans or signs of liquor for this very reason.

After a couple more minutes of talking, Sarah wanted to see Steven's room and make sure he had everything a kid would need. So far, Sarah was impressed with what she has seen and talked to Elaine about and she could not find anything against Steven's parents.

"May I see Steven's room?"

"Sure," Elaine said happily. Elaine was not offended. In fact, she was pleased with how well they were doing in keeping Sarah from finding anything wrong. Elaine loved Steven dearly and she knew that Joe did too. Yes, they both have their problems, but they both cared deeply for Steven and did not want to lose him to foster care.

Elaine walked Sarah to Stevens room.

"Here it is—a typical boy's room I would say." Sarah looked inside and did not see anything out of the ordinary. She saw a nice-looking twin bed in a corner, with a blue, metal bedframe. On top of the bed was a nice Kansas City Royals comforter, with a Royals pillowcase. The room was very clean, and Sarah saw that there was a TV with a couple of game systems underneath the cabinet that the TV sat on. There were dozens of video games Sarah noted, but she did not think that was anything wrong, Steven had mentioned that he loves to play video games. In the middle of the room was a light blue chair that seemed a little worn, but it looked big and comfortable. There were some toy boxes behind the chair and in the middle of the floor was a royal blue area rug between the chair and TV cabinet. Sarah was impressed with the cleanliness of the room and did not see anything wrong. In fact, she was surprised to see a decent chair in a kid's bedroom. In most cases, she would see just a small TV and a bed. They were lucky to even have a box spring. Sarah was beginning to doubt there was anything wrong and began to think about dropping the case.

"Well, thank you so much for everything, Elaine. I see that Steven is well taken care of and seems to be in a caring home."

"Thank you for the compliment. We try very hard to make sure that Steven has a good home environment."

"I can see that. Well, thank you so much for your time and you have a great day." Sarah began to walk towards the door and saw Jasmine sitting on the couch reading a book. "Have a great day, Jasmine, and a safe flight back home whenever you leave." Jasmine just looked over her book and gave Sarah a smile. That was the last chance Sarah had to see if Jasmine was covering for Elaine over the phone, but without that last bit of evidence, she walked to her car and left.

Elaine had been home for five months and it was September. Steven was surprised to see his mom home when he came back from school back in April. The last five months were beginning to brighten for Steven. Over the summer, he spent time with his mother and he realized that she did truly love him. He still had nightmares about the episodes he had witnessed, but he really wanted to have a relationship with one of his parents. Since his dad was hardly home, his mom was. At first, it was hard for Steven to open up to his mother. Usually after about a month, she would get "sick" as his dad would call it and go back to the hospital or drift in and out of halfway homes. But this time it was different. When his mom was home for longer than a month, she was usually quiet or watched soap operas all day. She would cook dinner and then watch TV in her bedroom, until his dad would finally come to bed. This time she was happier, and she always asked Steven if he would like to go out to eat for lunch or she would take him to the mall to shop for new video games. Steven loved getting new video games and that summer he played a new game every other week, thanks to his mom. His mom's cooking was getting really good and Steven looked forward to the dinners that she would make. She would make everything from scratch, and she took her time cooking it.

Steven also started middle school which helped him. Since the new school was a combination of other schools and nearly half of his old school mates went to other schools, not very many kids knew much about his home life. Also, Tanner Down went to another school and Zack was in this school, so it made Steven happy. He felt he had a fresh start and was beginning to feel comfortable with his mom at home. Steven still played a lot of video games when he got home but he did eat with his mom in the living room and talked to her about his days at school. He did not talk much to her, but he felt comfortable enough to at least give her an overview of how he was doing at school.

The other thing that made Steven happy and feel a little bit normal is that Mrs. Schmidt, or any other adult, had stopped pulling him away from lunch to talk about his home life. When he first started middle school in early August, he thought that maybe Mrs. Schmidt did not come, because she only worked at the elementary school. However, after almost two months at his new school, no one had come to talk to Steven about his home life whatsoever.

The only thing that Steven really disliked was that he did not get to spend any time with his dad. His dad would still come home at around eight p.m., eat whatever leftovers there were from that night's dinner, drink his beer and watch the news or sports highlights. His dad only had Sundays off, but he spent his day watching sports. Once in a while, his dad would play catch with him or talk to him but it was not very often.

Joe loved Steven, but he worked a lot, and drank a lot. His dad was not physically abusive towards Steven, but if Steven slipped in his grades or did something the slightest bit wrong at school, he would yell at Steven with such a fury that the windows seemed to shake in fright. Steven would just tear up and say, "Yes, Dad," and go to his room and play his games. His dad would eventually come to Steven and apologize and explain why he needed to raise his grades or why he acted a certain way at school and how it was not right. Overall, Steven still had decent grades in his classes but his dad would get angry if he slipped into a low C. He wanted to make sure that his son never dipped into D's, or lower, mainly for fear that a social worker would come snooping around again, since he knew that they oftentimes look at the students grades to see if anything is wrong at home. When they did talk, it was usually in the mornings when Joe dropped off Steven at school on his way to work. This was really the only time Steven ever got to talk to his dad and the ride was only fifteen minutes, so they did not get to talk much.

Other than time not spent with his father, Steven was happy that his life seemed to be normal. He was making some new friends at school. Yet, he would never invite them over to his house, just in case his mother had an episode or his dad came home drinking. He also did not go to friend's houses to avoid talking to their parents, in case if they knew his mother or father. He enjoyed his friends at school and wanted to keep it that way. Other than that, Steven was happy the way his life was finally going.

On a cool, October afternoon, Steven was walking home from school. He enjoyed walking home by himself when Zack was off at his football tryouts. Zack has tried to convince Steven for two months to join the football team, but Steven did not really like football or even watching it. Steven had lately grown out of sports in general and had been become interested in writing. He still liked to play his video games a fair amount of time but lately at school and sometimes before he went to bed, he liked to write short stories to help him escape his reality. Even though his life seemed to be getting better lately, he still had nightmares of his mom and his mom and dad fought all the time. When Joe got home and the house was not cleaned in the way he liked it, he got angry and started yelling at Elaine. Joe has not hit Elaine, but his temper can get so bad that the neighbors can hear his yelling from down the street. The police are never called because they know that Joe has never hit Elaine. By the time someone is ready to call for a noise disturbance, Elaine has calmed Joe down enough to stop yelling and has diverted his attention to either the TV or has offered him a beer which he will take and sit down while stewing over their recent argument. Steven always hates it when his dad yells at either him or his mother. He knows in the end his dad always apologizes to him, but his dad hardly apologizes to his mother. Also, his yelling can be so daunting, it scares Steven and that is why he usually locks himself up in his room.

Today is a cool day but the sun is out and casting brilliant warmth and light onto the changing trees. Steven notices that the trees are turning a beautiful, burnt orange color and then spots a tree with bright red leaves waving in the gentle breeze. A smell of fall brushes his nose, a sweet smell of decaying leaves and wet soil; he has always loved the sweet smell of fall. As he rode less than a block away from his house, he could hear his mother and father fighting down the street. Steven is wondering what his dad is doing home early; his dad always came home no earlier than eight in the evening. When he gets closer, he can hear his father and mother screaming.

"You stupid bitch, why don't you have the house clean?"

"I told you, Joe, that I have been washing clothes and the dishes all day. I was behind on those and at the same time I have been preparing dinner all day."

"I want the house spotless when I get home!" Joe yelled, showing Elaine that there was trash lying on the kitchen floor.

"When you get home? You don't usually get home till eight, why are you home now by the way?" Elaine yelled back at Joe.

"None of your business. I got off early is all." Joe then headed to the fridge to grab a few beers.

"Let me guess, you got fired again, didn't you?" Joe flinched at the word fired and his eyes grew with intense fire.

"No, I decided to quit." Then he opened a beer and began drinking it; halfway through, he set it down. "I hated that job."

"No, you seemed to like it, Joe, you seemed happier; you did not quit like the other jobs you were fired from, because you were drunk on the job again, weren't you!" Elaine struck a chord in Joe. Joe always told her he had quit his jobs, but she was right, he lost his jobs, because he would get caught drinking on the job. Usually, he got a warning at most of them, but he would get caught again and then fired. This job was a little more forgiving by giving him three warnings till they found him today, the fourth time, and fired him.

"No, I did not get fired! Who the hell told you that anyways?"

"Oh, word gets around, trust me."

"Trust you, I can't trust you as far as I can throw you. No one told you anything." Joe got up and walked towards Elaine.

"What, you going to hit me? Go ahead, try it, I will get CPS on your ass faster than before." Joe's eyes grew wide.

"You! You were the one who tipped them off about my drinking, wasn't it? I always thought they were snooping around because of you, but you told them about my drinking didn't you!"

"No Joe, I did . . ." but before Elaine could finish her words, Joe came towards her. Out of fear that Joe would possibly attack her, she ran towards the front door. Joe up to this point had never hit her, but she had at times felt that one day he would, and today she felt he would.

Elaine ran past Joe and towards the front door. "Where are you going? I am not through talking to you, Elaine!" Joe turned around and began walking towards her directly; she turned around to face him but she reached the end of the porch and did not notice that she walked backwards off the top step. Suddenly, she felt that she was falling and turned around to catch herself, but it was too late. Her leg got caught on the wooden terrace next to the step and she fell down the steps, with her right foot caught in the lattice. She felt a tremendous, sharp pain shoot through her leg and immediately saw that her leg was twisted halfway around. She saw blood coming down her shin and saw that her bone was bulging under the skin. She fainted at the sight of the broken leg.

Joe ran outside yelling, "Elaine, Elaine, are you okay?" Joe was panicking; he was afraid that people were going to think he beat Elaine up and caused this. He was not going to attack Elaine; he was moving closer to her face to intimidate her and see if she was the one who tipped CPS about his drinking. He cared for Elaine and was freaking out seeing her sprawled out on the ground, with a broken leg. He saw Cathy running across the street.

"Joe what the hell did you do?"

"I didn't do anything."

"I heard you guys arguing across the street and it sound pretty bad, are you sure you did not do anything to her?" Cathy was angry. Over the years, she was beginning to not like Joe. Elaine has confided in Cathy that they argued a lot, but reassured her that Joe had never hit her, but Cathy did not always believe it. At the same time, Elaine never had bruises on her that Cathy could see and Elaine usually wore t-shirts, with a skirt or dress, so Cathy always took her word for it. Joe looked around to see if anyone was outside to see the spectacle. He was growing both panicky and angry. He hated to feel embarrassed but now with Elaine on the ground, with a broken leg, he was afraid people would think he did this, by pushing her down the stairs. When Joe looked around, he saw Steven running down the sidewalk yelling, "Mom! Mom!"

"There you are, Steven. Cathy, I'm sure Steven saw the whole thing, didn't you son?" Steven ran up next to his mom and saw the broken leg. He immediately looked over to the side to hide his sudden nausea. "Steven, did you hear me, you saw what happened, right?" Steven looked up at his dad and then Cathy.

"Yeah, I saw it, but first call 9-1-1."

"Don't worry, Steven, I called the ambulance, after she fell and before I ran over here."

"Oh, okay. Thank you, Cathy." Cathy looked at Steven and gave him a hug.

"She'll be alright, Steven."

"But why is she not up?" Steven said with tears growing in his eyes.

"She fainted, after she saw her bone bulging under her skin; she didn't get knocked unconscious from the fall, she didn't hit her head," Joe said while leaning next to Elaine, with tears in his eyes. Under his breath he whispered, "I am sorry for yelling at you." But neither Steven nor Cathy heard him.

The ambulance arrived and Steven told the paramedics and Cathy what he had witnessed. That when he was down the street, he did hear his mother and father having an argument but he did not see his dad on the porch with his mom. He saw that his mom was walking backwards and tripped down the stairs, with her leg caught in the lattice of the porch. The paramedics looked her over and didn't see any bruises except where her leg was broken and, on her stomach, where she landed on the bottom step. The police arrived and Steven told them the same thing. They talked to the paramedics and both agreed that Joe was innocent of causing the accident; they did warn him that if they get another phone call for an argument, they will give him a ticket for public disturbance. They wanted to bust him for public intoxication but since he was in his house on his property, they could not do anything. But they did warn him that if he was ever caught intoxicated anywhere off the property, they would place him in jail for forty-eight hours. Joe thanked the officers and paramedics and asked to join Elaine in the back of the ambulance.

"Cathy, is it okay if Steven stays with you for dinner?" Joe said, as he climbed into the back of the ambulance.

"Sure thing, let me know how Elaine is doing when you get home, okay?"

"I will, thank you, Cathy." Then he entered the back of the

ambulance and sat next to Elaine. As Steven walked across the street with Cathy, he heard the sirens sound off into the distance.

On a cold and gloomy, January morning, Steven was playing the last bit of video games he could, on his last day of winter break from school. It has been nearly three months since his mother broke her leg. During this time, Steven had learned a lot about his parents. Steven learned that his mother did not leave her job because of wanting to be a stay-at-home mother, but because she was now collecting social security for her mental illnesses. Part of the deal that allows her to maintain her income is that she must attend a program for at least five years on an average of three days a week. The program is called CARE or Creating A Resource for Everyone. It is a program that helps people by monitoring them and making sure they have the resources they need to function in society on their own. Elaine does really well when she is not having an episode, but since her episodes are major, social security feels that in order to receive her benefits, she must attend CARE and also see a psychiatrist a minimum of four times a year.

Joe got a new job at an Italian restaurant called Antonio's. Joe worked a little less at his new job and lately Joe and Steven had been able to spend some time together; it has not been much time, usually they will talk about school or watch some sports together, but Steven did enjoy finally being able to spend time with his father. Steven beforehand would never have been able to watch sports with his dad and talk during the games. Usually, his dad would tell him to be quiet and just watch the game, but lately his dad has been in a good mood and they would talk during games. Steven did not like sports as much anymore, so their talks would be short, but, nevertheless, Steven liked being able to spend time with his dad, even if it was small talk and watching TV. Joe still drank a lot, but he mainly drank at home now. He was better at not drinking on the job anymore. Steven thought his dad's happier mood when he comes home was not only because he returned earlier than most of his other jobs, but because Joe was sober when he got home, since he didn't drink at work. Of course, over time, Joe would drink enough until his mood changed but it was close enough to Steven's bedtime that Steven did not notice the change, until later at night, but by then Steven was in his room playing games or writing.

"Steven?" Elaine was calling out from her bedroom. Steven got up and went to check on his mom. Elaine has been slowly getting better from her accident. She had surgery immediately when it happened, and the surgery went well. Her leg had to have rods placed and she has had to attend rehab to help gain strength back in her leg, because when the bone broke it severed some nerves. Elaine still had to rely on crutches, because she could not still put her full weight on her leg. The doctors say it will be another three to six months before she can walk on the leg without any support whatsoever. Lately, Elaine had seemed depressed and Steven figured it was because his mom could not get around much. She was picked up by a carrier service that CARE provides, since her leg was broken. She could hardly drive, because, if she is not doing rehab, she has to keep a cast on, and it extends her leg completely out.

Steven walked into the bedroom and noticed pill bottles laying on Elaine's nightstand. He noticed that they were full.

"Mom, have you been taking your meds?"

"Yes," Elaine answered in a low voice.

"Why are those pill bottles full then?" Steven walked closer to see which meds they were.

When he started to come closer Elaine rolled over and put them in the drawer.

"Oh, these are my pain medications, I don't take these because I do not want to get addicted to them." Then she rolled back over to look at Steven.

"Okay," Steven said in a low tone, almost low enough that Elaine could barely hear him. "What did you want, Mom?"

"I was wondering if you could grab my bible from the closet for me. It should be on the left side on the top shelf. Can you please bring it to me?"

His mom looked at him, but Steven felt something was not right. He knew his family was Catholic, but they were not particularly devoted. His parents never went to church and the only time that they do was when Jasmine was visiting and on holidays like Christmas and Easter. Steven thought it was odd his mother wanted to read the bible all of the sudden, but he went to the closet and found it. It was an old, worn bible made of what looked like once dark brown leather, but it was now faded. Steven saw that the pages were tipped with gold all around but due to the books age there was some spots where the gold was flaking off. He walked over and handed it to his mom. "Thanks, honey, this was Uncle Terry's bible."

She smiled at Steven and then opened the book and began reading. Once Steven heard his uncle's name, he began to panic. He remembered his mom's last major episode and Terry was the main subject during the episode. He was hoping his mom was not seeing him again.

"Is there anything else you need?" Steven asked wanting to see if he could fish out something from his mom.

"No, this is all I needed. My leg is really sore today and I did not want to get up. Thank you, honey, you can go back and play now." Elaine went back to reading her bible.

"Okay, just let me know if you need anything else." Steven stood there to see if she would respond but she just nodded her head to indicate okay and did not say anything else. Steven walked out of the room and went back to his room. He wanted to tell his dad that he felt something was wrong with his mom, but his dad was still at work. So, Steven went back to writing instead and waited until his dad got home to tell him.

Joe got home at six o'clock and seemed to be in a good mood. Steven did not want to tell his dad his suspicions, because he was afraid how his dad would react. His dad did not like to talk about his mother's condition and usually would ignore the conversation or reroute it to a different topic. Steven decided it was best to tell his dad, so he walked over to his dad right when he was opening a beer.

"Hey, Dad, can I tell you something?"

"Sure, Steven, what's up?" Joe placed his beer on the coaster that sat on the coffee table in front of the couch. He then turned on the TV to the sports highlights of the day.

"It's about mom." Joe looked over at Steven and Steven

flinched, worried what his dad might say.

"What's up?" Joe said looking Steven straight in his blue eyes.

"Well, Mom is acting differently today." Steven looked down at his legs and noticed he was shaking them mildly.

"How is she acting different?"

"Well today, she asked for a bible to read."

"Well that is not too different, she is probably bored, since she cannot do much other than CARE and rehab." Joe then looked back at the TV. Steven was surprised, he thought his dad would have acted differently or have taken it badly—but he didn't.

"Well, she said it was Uncle Terry's bible." Joe looked over to his son.

"Really?"

"Yeah"

"Did she say anything else?" Joe himself was beginning to grow a little worried; he remembered everything that had happened after Terry's death and Elaine's episode afterwards.

"No, she did not say anything else mentioning him, just telling me it was his bible."

Joe looked down at the floor then brushed his hair with his hand. He had not noticed anything different lately about Elaine. He always asked her if she had taken her meds and when he was asking about meds, he was referring to her psyche meds. She would take them in front of him most of the time and the other times he took her word for it, but she has been acting normally even after her accident. Joe was getting comfortable with Elaine and let up on her, since he felt guilty knowing that her leg was broken because of their fight.

"Well, I don't think there is anything to worry about Steven; as long as she hasn't mentioned that she has seen or heard Terry, she should be fine."

"Yeah, but haven't you noticed she seems a little more depressed."

"Yeah, but she is recovering from a really, bad, leg break and I honestly think it is from being cooped up in the house." Joe then went back to watching TV.

"Well, if you think it is okay, I guess I'll leave it alone." Joe looked at Steven.

"Steven, if you do notice anything different, let me know, but I think for right now your mom is okay."

"Okay, Dad." Then Steven went to his room and got his backpack ready for school for tomorrow.

A week had passed and Steven had noticed his mother's mood and personality had changed. Over the week, his mom would not talk to either him or his dad. She would just sit in her room and read her bible all day. The day after she asked Steven for the Bible, she asked Joe for a notebook and a pen. Every morning, Steven would walk by his mom's room and notice a stack of papers on her nightstand, with writing all over them. He did not pay much attention to them at first, but the last two mornings, he noticed the papers strewn across the bed. Joe usually slept on the couch because Elaine would leave the light on to read; she would read until one or two in the morning and Joe did not want to fight with her about the light, so he did not notice as much as Steven did.

It was a Sunday morning and Joe had to go into work, because the assistant manager called in sick. Steven was home by himself, with his mom. He wanted to go next door and hang out with Zack but he did not want to leave his mom home alone. So, he went into the living room and watched some cartoons. Then he heard his mom call out to him.

"Steven, Steven, can you come here please?" His mom's voice sounded monotone and tired. Steven went to his mom and saw the papers laying all over the bed and floor. He saw writing on them but could not make out what they said, they looked like a completely new language to him.

"Yes, Mom?" His mom slowly looked at him and stared. He remembered that stare, she was staring towards him but not at him. "Mom, are you okay?" Elaine laid there looking at Steven then slowly said,

"There is a Mother Mary miniature bust in the closet where you found Terry's bible, can you please bring her to me?" Steven looked at his mom, then at the closet. He wanted to say something, but his mom interrupted his train of thought.

"Please, Steven, I need her." Steven wanted to back out of the room to call his dad, but he decided to do what she asked. He walked to the closet and found the statue. It was a small bust of Mother Mary. It was about five inches tall. It was only her neck up with her hands held out in prayer. Her eyes were closed, and the face was a powdered white while the clothes around her head and neck were a powdered blue. It felt cold and smooth in his hands. Something that should have brought solace and peace to Steven gave him a feeling of dread and despair—he knew something was not right.

"Here you go, Mom."

"Thank you, Steven, and bless you."

Steven has never heard his mom say "bless you" to anyone. Maybe it was because she was so devoted recently, but at the same time he felt that something was not right. "You're welcome."

Then he walked out of her bedroom; he felt uncomfortable and wished his dad was home. Steven went back to the living room and watched TV. When Joe got home, Steven went to him and told him everything that happened.

"Okay, Steven, I'll go check on her." Joe walked into the bedroom and saw the papers laid around the room. He picked one up and tried to read it but could not make out what it said, it did not look like any language he has ever seen. What he did notice was that every piece of paper had the same exact words or characters in the same order repeatedly. "Elaine, is everything okay?" He saw her laying there with the Mother Mary statue clasped between her hands. She was chanting something to herself. Joe noticed she had been in the same clothes all week. He never noticed, because whenever he saw her, she was under the blankets reading her bible. He noticed that her hair was dirty and oily. The light from the lamp next to her shined off her hair and he started to notice a sour smell. He was beginning to wonder if he had ever seen her get out of bed to use the bathroom. He walked up to her and noticed the smell was getting stronger. When he went to get closer to her, his foot hit against something and he felt his feet get wet. He looked down and saw urine and feces knocked onto the floor.

"What the hell, Elaine, have you been going to the bathroom in this bucket?" He began to grow nauseous from the smell, because after it was knocked over the smell hit his nose like a hammer. "I know you can get up; why have you been pissing and shitting in a bucket?" Elaine just laid there in the bed chanting. Joe could barely hear what she was chanting but he thought he heard her say, "I believe, I believe" over and over again.

"Elaine, get up and clean this shit up, it is disgusting. You have been laying around all day. The doctor said you are good enough to walk in this condition." But Elaine just stayed there chanting. "Elaine, I have been nice to you since your accident, and I have been sleeping on the couch so you can read all night, but you can at least speak up, so I can hear you better."

Elaine slowly looked over at Joe and began shaking the Mother Mary statue in her hands furiously and began yelling at Joe, "I BELIEVE, I BELIEVE!" Joe knew she must be having a start to an episode. He had not seen one completely yet. He has always showed up at the end of them or when she was being taken away from the police. He felt nervous and ran out of the room.

"Steven!"

"Yes, Dad, what's wrong, I heard Mom yelling."

"Yeah, she seems to be getting sick again, Steven."

Steven's heart began to pound, he knew it, he knew his mom was showing signs, but he was really hoping this would pass over.

"Should I call the police then?" Steven began to walk towards the telephone in the kitchen.

"No, do not call the police, I don't want people to know what is going on."

Joe was telling a part truth. He did not want the police showing up, because he did not want the neighbors to snoop around. He knew that if the police came, half of the block will be seeing the spectacle, and even if Elaine is tame enough, the sight of the cop cars is enough to drag people out of their homes. But the main reason he did not want police around is because he knew that if Elaine made a big scene, and police were involved, CPS would be back and he did not want to risk having that happen. Joe paced back and forth thinking.

"Okay, we will try to get her get in the truck and we will take her to the hospital."

"What if she does not agree?" Steven looked at his dad with tears in his eyes. Steven had been through these episodes and he hated them. He knew this would haunt him for nights to come.

"I don't know," Joe said to himself, "but I do not want the police involved this time. We need to take care of this ourselves."

Steven's heart began to pound; he had never tried asking his mom if she would want to go to the hospital. She was usually so far gone the police had to step in.

"Okay, Dad, we will try to get her into the truck." Then Steven walked next to his dad and they walked into the bedroom together.

Joe and Steven walked into the bedroom and Elaine was still laying there chanting, "I believe, I believe," while holding the Mother Mary firmly in her hands. Steven saw the papers laying all over the floor and noticed they had the same repetitive sayings written on all of them. He looked at them closely while his father talked to his mom.

"Elaine, we need to take you to get help. Come with me and Steven, okay?" Elaine just kept chanting to herself. Joe felt an eerie feeling. He was a catholic, but he was not by any means devout. He believed in God, but he did not attend church or pray; he just merely believed and that was all. Yet, he felt a presence he had never felt before and he did not know if it was his mind playing tricks on him, or it was the way Elaine was chanting to herself, with her blank stare looking forward.

"Dad, I realized something." Steven was tugging at his dad's shirt.

"What?" Joe looked down and saw Steven holding one of the papers in his hands.

"I looked at the papers closer and realized that it is not a strange language; it is I BELIEVE spelled backwards." Joe took the paper from Steven and looked at it. Joe grabbed a pen from his side of the bed and wrote down the words "I believe" then worked them backwards.

When he was finished writing, he saw that the words said "EVEILEBI" which is the exact phrase that is repeated on the hundreds of sheets of papers laying all over the bed and floor. Joe felt a shiver run down his back and looked at Steven.

"Steven, go back into the living room, I can try to do this myself, I don't want you to get hurt in case your mom attacks one of us." Joe then ushered his son out the room and closed the door.

Steven did not go into the living room; he stood next to the door to listen to his parents and to make sure his dad didn't need help.

"Elaine," Joe looked at Elaine for some kind of response. Lie there is all she did and continued chanting—that same chant that Joe was slowly growing to hate. It not only creeped him out but it made him angry, because he felt powerless. He knew she was gone mentally and that he would have to physically get her out of the room. That is why he wanted Steven out of the room, just in case he got in the way.

"Elaine, answer me, we need to get you help, you are freaking me and Steven out." He motioned closer to Elaine. To Joe's surprise, Elaine stopped chanting and looked at Joe.

"Elaine, let's get you ready and let us get you help." Elaine turned her head slowly without blinking. She held on to the statue. Only her head moved, her body was still. Joe noticed her breathing was shallow and that her skin looked pale. Joe began to inch closer to Elaine.

"GET OUT!" Elaine, despite her healing, broken leg, lunged out of the bed towards Joe. She crawled out of the bed like a demon possessed and with the statue in one hand, she tried to grab Joe by the throat. Joe backed up and ran towards the door. Elaine managed to grab Joe's shirttail and nearly toppled him to the floor. Joe managed to grab the doorknob for leverage and called out for Steven. Immediately, Steven opened the door and grabbed his father's hand and pulled his father towards him. Joe took off his shirt and closed the door right before Elaine could get her hand past it. Joe grabbed the door handle and held it tight. To his surprise, Elaine did not try to open the door. He listened closely to the door and could hear a faint, "I believe, I believe," on the other side.

"Dad what happened?" Steven was panicky, he knew what it was like to be on the other end of his mother's wrath.

"I don't know, she just snapped. She yelled at me to get out and attacked me." Joe walked over to the dryer in the washroom and grabbed a shirt.

"Should I call the cops now?" Steven looked towards the phone in the kitchen.

"No, no cops."

"Well, what are we going to do then, Dad?" Steven was scared; he just wanted this over, before anything else happened.

"I have an idea, Steven, which will keep the police away and not disturb the neighbors." Joe then grabbed a beer out of the fridge and drank it all at once, then grabbed another one and sat down on the couch.

"What is it, Dad?" Joe looked at Steven and sighed. He was quiet and Steven did not like it. Then his dad finally spoke after rubbing his hands through his sweaty, black hair.

"Well, today is Sunday, which means tomorrow your mom will be going to a CARE meeting, since she goes Monday, Wednesdays, and Fridays. Well, since they have transportation for her, I think that will be our way of getting her out of here without the police involved."

Steven's heart began to pound. He looked at the clock and saw that it was seven. "So, we will have to wait thirteen hours?" Steven said to his father while still staring at the clock.

"Yeah, it is the only thing I can think of."

"What if she tries to attack the driver, or she runs past the door or something?"

"Well, we will have to see, Steven, okay. I did not say it was a perfect plan, but we have to try something without involving the police."

"Okay . . . well I am going to make a sandwich and go to my room, I guess."

"Yeah, you should go do that. When she yelled at me saying, 'get out,' I think she wants to be alone. I am hoping she will stay in the room all night, I mean she has not come out of her room for over a week, so I don't think this night will be any different." Joe deep down was praying for the first time in years that what he was saying would come true.

Steven went into his room and began to play video games. It helped keep his mind off his mom. Deep down, he was torn apart. He really hoped that this time it was different. Everything was going right for once and now his mom was getting sick again. He knew that after this she will probably be gone for a long time and he would miss her. Whenever she was gone, he missed her because she was his mom, but this time he felt like he would miss her because he enjoyed having her home. He wanted to know why she got sick this time. He knew that in the past they did not have the right medications for her but this time it seemed like they got it right. She was doing really well and she seemed happy and outgoing. Steven just kept playing his game, until it was time to go to bed. Steven turned off the TV and laid in bed hoping that this night would go by like any other night.

Steven fell asleep fitfully. It took him two hours to finally fall asleep by around midnight. He finally drifted off. An hour later, he woke up from what he believed was a nightmare.

He thought his mother was in the room with him. Steven opened his eyes to darkness. Steven never slept with a light on because it kept him up and he always kept his blinds closed so he could sleep in complete darkness. He always felt that the complete darkness helped keep his mind from over thinking and believed that it helped keep his mind clear of nightmares.

When Steven fully awakened, he felt an odd presence in his room. He already felt on edge knowing his mom was having an episode, but he really felt like someone was in the room with him. He tried to get his eyes to adjust to the darkness but there was not a sliver of light to help his eyes adjust to his surroundings. He rubbed his eyes hoping it would help, but it was no use—he was still staring into complete darkness. He closed his eyes and sat still; he was afraid to move, in fear that someone was really there. Steven began to think that maybe he did not really wake up and he was still dreaming. So, he sat there and held his breath so he could hear his surroundings. Then Steven heard very low breathing and the hairs on his body stood up. He froze and now knew someone was in the room with him. Steven hoped it was maybe his father checking in on him. "Dad?" Steven whispered. There was no response. "Dad, is that you?"

Steven raised his voice a little, thinking maybe his dad did not hear him the first time. There still was no answer. Steven was beginning to get scared. He then yelled out, "DAD!" at the top of his lungs.

Suddenly, Steven's bedroom door flew open and Steven saw his dad turn on the light; when Steven looked down, he saw his mom standing there with her eyes closed, with the Mother

Mary statue in one hand while her other hand was stretched out over the foot of Steven's bed. Steven screamed and jumped out of bed, running towards his dad.

"Elaine what the hell are you doing?" Joe yelled at Elaine and then caught Steven in his arms. "Steven, are you okay?" Steven hugged his dad tightly and smelled the alcohol on his dad's breath. Steven did not care; he was just glad his dad came in. "Steven go lay down in the brown recliner, okay?" Steven nodded and walked off towards the living room.

Elaine turned around and looked at Joe. She said nothing and just stared at Joe.

"Elaine, what the hell were you doing? You scared Steven." Elaine's eyes opened wide and she pointed her pale finger towards Joe.

"Hell is where you are going, if you do not believe!" Joe was struck frozen. Part of it was shock at what she said and the other part was it was something different than the chant she had been repeating.

"Elaine, get out of Steven's room now and go to bed." Elaine stood there and then held out the Mother Mary statue towards Joe.

"He who believes will be saved!" Then she slowly walked towards Joe.

Joe did not know what to do, he wanted to go to Elaine and try a nicer route. He thought that maybe if he tried to console her, maybe she would cooperate. He slowly walked towards Elaine, as she walked towards him. Soon, the statue was lightly pressing against Joe. He stopped and was frozen. He wanted to try to get closer to Elaine, but she kept her arm extended, with the statue between them. Then she yelled out, "LET HE WHO IS TOUCHED BE SAVED!"

Then she pressed the statue into Joe's chest and he fell backwards. Joe landed straight on his back but he kept his head up high enough so that he did not hit the floor with it. Elaine then stood right over Joe and closed her eyes and started chanting, "Do you believe, do you believe?"

Joe just stared at her; he did not want to grab her or do anything that would make it look like they had a fight. Also, Joe realized she was not really attacking him, but he was still nervous; he did not know what she was going to do. He laid there for a minute and then he had an idea.

"I do believe." Joe said out loud. Elaine stopped chanting at Joe and then stepped over him. Joe laid on the floor and watched Elaine walk away. He was not entirely sure it was going to work but he thought if he just went along maybe she would be satisfied. Joe then saw that Elaine went into the living room and sat on the couch staring at Steven. Steven sat there looking at his mother who was unresponsive. Steven was too scared to say anything, and he was afraid if he did, his mom would do something. So, Steven just sat there, motionless, looking at his mom, while she just stared at him, chanting her "I believe" mantra. Joe came into the living room and sat down in the second recliner.

"Steven, just tell her you believe too and she will leave you alone."

Steven looked at his father and nodded. Then Steven looked at his mom holding the statue between her hands while she was chanting. He got up out of his chair and slowly walked towards his mother. The living room was only lit by the illumination from the TV that his dad was watching during the night. When Steven got closer, he noticed his mother's eyes were closed and that she was gently rocking in the rocker recliner. Steven inched closer to his mother and then her eyes opened wide and she looked at Steven.

"Do you believe?" she asked him. Steven looked at his dad and his dad nodded at him to just say yes. Steven looked back at his mom and choked out "Yes, I believe." Elaine extended the statue out and touched Steven on the chest. Steven could feel the hard and stony figure press into his chest. Then his mom said, "You are saved, my son!" and then she fell into the chair and went to sleep.

Steven sighed and began walking back to his bedroom then he heard his dad call out to him.

"Steven, stay in here tonight, I have a feeling the night is not over."

"Why is that?" Steven said tiredly.

"She may seem asleep, but we need to stay up all night and watch her just to make sure."

"But I have school in the morning, I need to go to sleep."

"Don't worry, I will call you out sick in the morning, okay?" Steven did not mind school, but after what happened tonight, he would like to be able to just stay home and play games or write to keep his mind off of things.

"Okay, Dad, sure." Steven walked over to the recliner and sat there and watched T.V. with his dad.

At three in the morning, his dad got up from the couch. Steven heard his dad go to the fridge and open a beer. Then, his dad went to a cabinet and grabbed something. When his dad came back into the living room, Steven saw his dad holding gold bells. They looked like shining golden grapes and Steven was curious as to why his dad was holding them.

"Dad, what do you have?" Joe put his beer down on the coffee table quietly and walked over to Steven.

"Hey, try to keep your voice down," Joe whispered. "Try not to wake your mom up okay?"

"Okay, sorry," Steven whispered back. "Anyways, what are those for?" Steven pointed towards the bells.

"I am going to hang these up on the front doorknob, in case your mom tries going outside."

"What about the back door?"

"Don't worry about the back door; the chair your mom is in is right by the door and that is the door she is most likely to go out of if she leaves."

"I thought we were going to stay up all night though?"

"Yeah, but I can tell you are getting tired and, honestly, I am tired too and this is just in case we both fall asleep."

"Do you think she will try to leave? She seems to be pretty interested in us, Dad."

"Yeah, but to her we both are saved, what if she wants to save other people, too?" Steven looked down and knew his dad was right. Also, Steven knew his mom always liked to run out of the house during an episode, but this episode seemed less intense than the other two. Steven knew well enough that anything could happen with his mom.

Joe tied the bells around the doorknob quietly. Steven was impressed on how quietly his dad was able to do it; he did not hear one bell jingle at all. Joe went back to the couch and started to watch TV. An hour passed by and Steven was drifting in and out of sleep. Soon, Steven closed his eyes and he was awakened by snoring from his dad.

"Oh man, dad is asleep, I wonder if I should wake him up." Steven looked at his mom and saw that she was still asleep.

"Well, I guess I should let him sleep; looks like mom is still out." Steven looked back at the TV and the repeat of the news played over again. Steven fought for another thirty minutes and then fell deeply asleep.

Steven was startled awake, by the sound of bells ringing violently. Steven looked over and saw that the clock said six a.m. He turned over and saw his dad jump up and run towards his mother who was sprawled on the floor, desperately trying to open the door. Steven remembered that the whole night his mom was not using crutches and she must have hurt her leg again or she must be in pain from the leg.

"Let me out, I have to go save the others!" Elaine was screaming at the top of her lungs now. Joe ran towards her and grabbed her.

"LET ME GO!" Elaine shoved Joe off and he fell back.

"Dad, what do you want me to do?" Steven yelled at his dad, but his dad told him,

"Don't do anything, I'll handle it." Honestly, Steven would be of no use; he knew how strong his mom could be when she is sick like this and he was barely turning eleven next month. Also, Steven was too scared to really move; he just saw the whole thing play out before him. His mother screaming and holding on to the door while his dad repeatedly tried to lift her up to bring her to the chair—each time a failed attempt.

"Elaine, stop or you are going to wake up the neighbors!" Joe tried again to grab Elaine, but her strength was incredible; Joe felt like he was trying to subdue a bear. Joe then rethought his approach and tried a different tactic. "Elaine, how about you . . . I mean we try to save other's later today?" Elaine stopped screaming and looked at Joe. She did not say anything, but Joe knew he must have gotten to her somehow.

"How about we wait till later this morning and we can go out together and try to save as many people we can, okay? Let's get back to the chair so you can rest and prepare." Joe held his hand out to Elaine. She looked at him, it seemed to have worked. She nodded at Joe and got up. Joe led her to the chair and sat her down. She began to chant "We will save all" over and over again, until eight in the morning.

CARE transportation arrived and Steven was exhausted. To his surprise, his father's plan worked. Joe told the transportation driver everything that happened. The driver told Joe that CARE does provide outpatient services but if the patient needs to be referred to impatient help, they can do that. Joe convinced Elaine that the driver was going to take her on a trip to help save other people. Elaine seemed reluctant at first but the driver played along with the ruse. When Elaine was convinced that the driver was going to save people with her; she agreed to get into the van.

Steven watched as his mother walked into the van; she still held on to the Mother Mary statue firmly in her hands, and was still chanting to herself. He could not hear her, but he knew that she was repeating a mantra to herself. Steven heard his dad call his school and Steven went to his room. Joe then called Jasmine to tell her what happened.

"What, you can't come and watch Steven?" Joe was too tired to try and to convince his mom to come to Kansas. He knew she was getting up in age and that she would not be able to come after every episode.

"Okay, thanks anyways, Mom, I love you; I'll let you know what happens." Joe then hung up the phone and then called into work. That day both Steven and Joe slept the whole day away.

EPISODE FOUR

Over a year had passed since Elaine has come home from her last episode. She only spent about six months away from home this time. Steven found out that her last episode was not caused as a result of a wrong mix of medication. Elaine was doing really well, until the last episode. After Elaine went away, Joe went into the bedroom to clean up the mess that was left behind. Joe had to keep from throwing up due to the smell from all the feces and urine that Elaine collected in a plastic tub hidden under the bed. As Joe was cleaning up the mess, he noticed there were pills laying all over the bottom of the nightstand and that the pill bottles were strewn all over along with the pills. He saw that the pills seemed to have been slightly dissolved. He picked several up and looked at them closely and saw that the identification numbers were partially missing which meant they were wet at some point, and when he looked even closer, he could see residue on the pills that looked like dried powder. Joe figured out what happened to these pills. Elaine must have been acting like she took her pills. Joe would ask her if she took them and he would often times see her take them in front of him, but he never looked in her mouth. Joe realized that she was not really taking her pills and that she was putting them in her mouth and acting like she was taking them. Then once Joe left, she then spit them out and hid them back in the pill bottles or simply threw them into the bottom of the nightstand drawer. Joe was both angry at Elaine and himself. He did love Elaine and he wanted to see her well, but he felt like she was lying to him this whole time. He would ask her if she took her pills and even watched her several times, but behind his back, she was not taking them. Joe felt angry at himself for not following up, he should have tried harder to verify that she was in fact taking them, but he never thought about her fake swallowing pills. Joe told Steven about the pills because he wanted his son to know for future reference. When Elaine comes back home, both Joe and Steven will have to make sure she is taking her medications.

When Elaine finally returned, Steven was not as excited as he hoped. After the last accident, he had become more reclusive from his friends at school and would shut himself up in his room more so than before. Beforehand, he would talk to his dad or spend some time with his mom, but he did not want anything to do with either of them. Steven experienced more nightmares to the extent that they now happened every night. Steven's grades were starting to slip at school, because he was so tired all the time. His nightmares haunted him to the point where he went to bed late, because he thought that, the later he went to sleep, the less time he would have to dream.

Steven's physical depreciation was starting to show, not to the extreme that CPS would get involved, but enough where it was brought up at the last teacher's conference with his father. Steven's eyes were beginning to look sunken. The look of sadness was always a mask over Steven. He would come to class with his skin pale and with such dark, sunken eyes that he looked like he had been in a fight and was recovering from a weeks old, black eye. He would often times fall sleep in class and that was the main reason his grades were truly suffering.

Steven's home life was not in a terrible shape; it just went back to normal, after Elaine came back home recently. His mother got back on her meds and had stuck with them. Joe still had his same job at Antonio's and still had the same schedule. Steven thought that having everything back to normal would make him happy again, but he knew deep down nothing lasts for long with either of his parents. Steven was just waiting for the next episode to come around. He was waiting for his dad to lose this job and get a new one again and his schedule to change. Steven did not want to get comfortable, because he knew it could all change at any time.

It also did not help that Zack has gone on to high school. Steven was now in seventh-grade and Zack was two grades ahead of Steven. Also, during the two years at middle school, Zack was drifting off, because he joined the football team. Steven grew less interested in sports, so naturally, Steven and Zack did not hang out as much. Sometimes, they would play video games together, but Zack always wanted to practice for football and Steven did not like to play, so Steven would go home and do his own thing while Zack did his. But now that Zack was in high school, things had changed drastically between the two. Zack made new friends in high school and freshman were looked down upon, if they still hung out with middle school kids. If Steven had been in at least eighth grade, it would not have been as bad, but since Steven was still a seventh-grade student, Zack would be ridiculed and shunned by his new friends. Steven had made some new friends in the last two years, but he never really clicked well enough with them. They were friends enough to eat together at lunch or to talk, but never enough to discuss his home life, only Zack knew and that is why Steven took it hard when Zack left. Steven had no one to talk to about his home life or at least know that someone knew about it and understood. Steven never opened to anyone new, because he did not want anyone to know or to spread rumors. Since Elaine's last episode did not involve the cops, no one really knew what happened and Steven never worried about anyone making fun of him about his mother.

Then one day, everything changed for Steven when a new kid came to his school. The boy's name was Mike Adison. Mike came from a different school in the city. He was not an out-of-town kid; his mother moved across town due to a recent divorce and moved into the district. Mike was a quiet kid and did not have any striking features. He had long, sandy, blonde hair that went down to his shoulders and he did not look very athletic. Mike was about the same size as Steven but maybe just an inch or two taller. Their builds were about the same. When Steven saw him enter the first day in his math class, he did not pay much attention to Mike. After a week had passed, he noticed Mike was quiet and shy. Steven learned about Mike's parents splitting up and found out Mike was a single child. Steven started to grow interested in Mike, because it sounded like they both came from broken homes. Steven did not want to compare their shattered lives, but Steven did feel that Mike would be the closest person he knew that would share any resemblance of what it is like to come from similar messed up lives and each was an only child.

One day Steven saw that Mike was sitting at the 'every kid for themselves' table—the last table where either the outcasts sat or those who had no friends. Steven decided to sit next to Mike and just eat. He figured that if Mike would open up to him, he would talk, but Steven was definitely not the kid to strike up a conversation first. Steven sat next to Mike and ate his lunch silently. The smell of cafeteria pizza was lingering in the air and Steven noticed that Mike barely touched his food. It looked like he just piddled around with his pizza. Steven saw that Mike took out a piece of paper from his pocket and began to write on it. Steven tried to see what Mike was writing, but Mike's head was directly over it in concentration. His long, blonde hair engulfed his face and seemed to hide the paper. Steven wanted to see but couldn't. Steven just sat there quietly and finished his lunch. When the bell rang, Mike got up and for a second the paper was plain for all to see. Steven slyly glanced at the paper, before Mike realized it was still there and grabbed it, Steven saw that the top of the paper in big capital letters read "FALL BREEZE" and saw what looked like stanzas. Steven then realized that Mike was writing a poem and Steven thought to himself that they both had something in common, without a word ever spoken between them.

After a week of sitting next to Mike and neither one saying a word to each other, Steven finally suppressed his anxiety and decided to talk to Mike. Today was Salisbury steak day and Steven did not care much for it, so he thought today would be a good day to try to talk to Mike. He did not have to worry about eating in between conversations, in case one should exist. Steven sat down his tray and sat there. Steven thought it may be a good idea to try writing as well to show Mike that he also likes to write. When Steven brought out his pen and paper, Mike looked over and smiled. Luckily for Steven he did not have to start the conversation. "You like to write too?" Mike said. Steven had never really heard Mike talk and was surprised at how deep his voice was compared to Steven's. They were almost the same size and build, but it sounded like Mike was already an adult while Steven still had his twelve-year-old twang. "Yeah, I love to write, especially poetry, it always helps to clear your mind." Steven looked down at his paper, staring at the only word he wrote down—"THE." "I understand completely, after my parents separated, I really got into writing. Beforehand, I liked to write to do something productive, but now I write because it helps me through issues." Steven's heart jumped in excitement. He knew so well how much he had escaped to writing, in order to help forget about his home life.

"When did they separate?"

"Oh, about a year ago, but they lived with each other for about ten months until everything was official. They fought even worse during those ten months because they knew that since they were separating, they could yell at each other no matter how bad. They were still going to split in the end anyways." Mike sighed. "Sorry, I did not mean to lay all that on you, after our first interaction with each other." Mike blushed and looked away.

"Oh, don't worry about it, I have stuff that you would not believe." Then Steven stopped talking immediately; he did not know what he just said. He was not ready to tell anyone about his past, yet at the same time he wondered that if he did, would it help? Would talking with someone about it and not just hiding behind a TV or paper help? Before Steven realized it, the bell rang and he had told Mike everything that had happened. Steven felt embarrassed; he could not believe what he just did, telling a complete stranger about his mom and dad, but he felt better. He felt he could breathe for the first time in his life; the only thing that was bothering him now is what Mike would think. Would Mike run away laughing, would he make fun of Steven? Steven realized he was sweating, and his heart was pounding—he felt he had made a huge mistake. For a minute, after the bell, they stood there in silence. Then Mike talked.

"Wow, I am glad that I am not the only one with a messed-up family." Steven just nodded and began to pick up his tray. "Hey, Steven, you want to come over sometime, maybe we could sit down and write together, you know, check each other's works or hang around and play video games?" Steven smiled and looked at Mike. "Yeah, I would like that. I would like that a lot." Then they parted ways and went to their classes.

It had been three months since Steven and Mike met but they were inseparable. They hung out every weekend together.

Steven had been spending the night over at Mike's once a week. Both of their parents did not mind, especially Joe. Joe was glad that Steven was getting out of the house and being social. Joe thought that maybe this would change Steven's grades around and they did. Steven was not having as many nightmares and having someone to talk to really helped clear his mind. Also, when Mike and Steven had their writing get together, sometimes they would talk new ideas and Steven would write them down on paper; it was a way to get things off his chest both verbally and physically. Steven's pallor improved. Since he had been able to sleep more, his sunken eyes looked less lifeless; not only that, his eyes seemed to sparkle with happiness. Steven and Mike were close and Steven enjoyed having a friend he felt comfortable with talking about his parents, and Steven did care for Mike too. He intently listened to Mike when he complained about how his dad had stopped coming to visit and how his mom was bitter towards everyone about the divorce, even towards Mike. Steven noticed it too. Mike's mom was never mean towards Steven, but she never really asked him about anything. It just seemed like she did not care that Steven was over or that he spent the night once a week. But Steven did not mind, in fact, he enjoyed it, because she never asked Steven anything; he did not have to worry about bringing up things about his parents. For these last three months, Steven was finally happy.

Steven was getting ready for school and looked forward to spending the night at Mike's. They decided that they would critique each other's poems together. They were even thinking of sending their works out to a contest, for the school library writing contest. It was not a big event, the prize was some free books and recognition, but they both felt it would be a great opportunity to see how well their works were valued. When Steven was getting ready, he heard his mother in the living room singing. He noticed that she was extra happy this morning and Steven did not pay any attention to it. She did not seem to be doing anything particularly weird.

"Hey, Mom." Steven saw that his mom had cut her hair short. Her once long, blonde hair that touched her once slim waist, was now short, but it looked nice on her. Elaine had gained some weight, during the year, due to her meds. She ate more now and he noticed that she ate more carb-oriented foods which is what his father told Steven. Joe told Steven one day that his mother will likely gain weight, because one of the side effects of her medications is weight gain, due to an increased craving of carbs. Joe wanted to tell Steven that it would be normal if Elaine gained weight and it did not mean she was more depressed or that it was a pre-curser to a possible episode. She still looked pretty for her age and, besides, the slight gain in weight, if anything, has helped keep her face plump and has kept wrinkles away by tightening the skin.

"Yes, Steven?" Elaine looked over at Steven, with a big smile across her face. Steven had not seen her this happy before, but he was glad that she was.

"Don't forget, I will be over at Mike's tonight, so don't make too much food."

"Oh, I know. Have fun, I'll see you tomorrow when you get home from his house." Then she began to sing to herself again. Steven wanted to ask her why she was so happy but noticed that it was getting late for school, so he left without saying anything else to his mom.

After school, Steven rode his bike with Mike back to Mike's house. Mike's mom was in the living room watching TV, with a bottle of vodka sitting on the coffee table. She looked tired and worn. Her black hair was placed in a ponytail, and her business suit was undone. It looked like she had a wet stain across it.

"Hey, Mom."

"Hey," is all Mike's mom said.

"Everything okay?"

"Yeah," she uttered staring at the TV.

"Don't forget Steven is staying over tonight, since it is Friday."

"I know, have fun." Then she took a swig from her bottle and laid down on the couch.

"Your mom, okay, Mike?"

"Yeah, she must have had another hard day at her job. She has been having issues with the new lawyer she works for and I guess he has hard and demanding clients, and since she is the only paralegal there, she is getting all the case load."

"Dang, that sucks."

"Yeah, but she will be okay, don't worry about her, she will be fine."

"Okay, but if you need anything else, Bro, I am here for you."

"I know, I appreciate it. Hey, let's start looking at each other's work."

"Okay, cool."

That whole evening, Steven and Mike critiqued each other's works. After they were done, they decided to play some video games together to decompress. While they were playing, Steven had this nagging feeling that there was something wrong back home. He kept playing back the morning in his head. He could not remember ever seeing his mother that happy before.

"Hey, Steven, you okay?" Mike paused the game.

"Yeah, why?"

"Well, for starters, the past half hour you have seemed spacey."

"Well, we are playing a game, sometimes I do that you know."

"I know, but usually you are kicking my ass in this fighting game, but tonight I have won every match. Usually, I am lucky to win two out of ten against you." Steven looked down and stared at his controller.

"Okay, you know me too well. This morning my mom seemed extra happy."

"Yeah, so, don't you have bouts of happiness from time to time?" Mike chuckled and slapped Steven on the shoulder.

"Yeah, but like small bouts, like after I write a piece, I felt helped me, or beating a hard level in a game, but she just seemed extra happy for no reason."

"Well, she is taking meds, maybe she just had an extra dose you don't know about or maybe her doctor changed them."

"Yeah, but when she is happy, it's because something happened to cause it."

"Bro, it was the morning, maybe she was just happy to be

happy. I would not worry about it."

"Yeah, maybe you are right." Mike un-paused the game and Steven began to drift off into thought.

No matter how much he could try to shake it off, Steven still had a feeling of dread looming over him. His mood was changing, and Mike could tell. Mike wanted to say something, but he felt that Steven would just agree to whatever he said and let it go, so Mike said nothing. Sometimes silence helps him out so he figured maybe Steven just needs some time to think to himself.

After they were done playing their game, Mike grabbed a pen and some paper and handed it to Steven.

"Here, maybe whatever you are thinking or feeling right now, you can write down on this paper. It does not even have to be a poem. Lately, I have been just writing down my feelings, just jotting down what comes to mind and it seems to help, especially with my mom lately."

Steven looked up at Mike.

"You told me earlier everything is fine with her."

"Yeah, but just because I think she is fine does not mean I still do not worry that something may happen like her losing her job or maybe she will take out her situation at work on me soon. She usually lashes out at me, just because I am the only one here. Since my dad is not around to yell at her and for her to yell back, I am the next person she yells at, hell, sometimes she just yells at me but not at *me*. If you know what I mean."

Mike was still holding on to the pen and paper and began to wave it at Steven while smiling. "Come on buddy, just write, I know it will help, okay?"

Steven looked at Mike and took the pen and paper.

"If you need me too, I will leave the room."

"No, that's okay, Mike, you can stay in here, it's your room anyways" Steven gave a slight laugh. Mike laughed back and gave a smirk.

"At a boy, get to writing and I'll just sit here and write myself, if you need to talk to me, let me know." Then they both sat there writing, till one in the morning.

When it was time to go to sleep, Steven laid there staring off into space. Mike fell asleep quickly and was lightly snoring. In the background, Steven could hear Mike's mom snoring heavily, from across the hall. It was loud enough to penetrate through two doors, because both Mike's and his mom's doors were closed. Steven was not awake because of the snoring, but he could not stop thinking about his mom—from this morning. He should be happy that she was in a really, great mood this morning, but he could not stop thinking of how happy she seemed. He could not stop thinking about her. He began to worry about his dad and how he was doing—was his mother getting sick again, is he fine by himself with her, or is she fine? Steven just laid there in the bed, staring at the ceiling.

The moon was half full and it was shining through a small sliver of the curtain. Mike usually kept his room fairly well lit, but Steven liked to sleep in the dark. So, they agreed to have the curtain slightly open for a compromise, so both of them could be happy. Even though it is Mike's house and he could have done what he wanted, Mike really enjoyed Steven as a friend and understood why Steven liked to sleep in the dark.

Steven wanted to make Mike happy and let some of the natural light of the night filter in. Usually, Steven could sleep in this setting, but tonight his thoughts about home kept him up.

Then it hit him, he sat straight up in the sleeping bag and uttered to himself, "She is getting sick!" He woke Mike up.

"Hey, what's up Steven?" Mike hit the button on his clock to light it up. "Bro, it's four in the morning, what's wrong?"

"I remembered!"

"Remembered what?" Mike laid back in his bed and closed his eyes half awake.

"I know what has kept me up this whole time." Mike rolled over and looked down at Steven laying in his sleeping bag, his eyes finally adjusting to the small amount of moonlight hitting Steven. Mike noticed that Steven did not sleep at all and he looked tired but energized. His hair was messy, and he noticed Steven was breathing a little fast.

"Whoa, you have been up this whole time?"

"Yeah, I've been thinking and thinking and could not help but feel this odd feeling about my mother, but now I remembered why I have felt this way all evening and night."

"Well, spit it out." Mike got down and sat next to Steven.

"The last time my mom was super happy like this was when I was almost four, when she had her first episode." Steven looked at Mike. "She is going to have another one, I can tell. She was super happy the first time she had one and I was really young when it happened. I barely remembered the start of it. I usually just remember the main part of the episode, but not what led up to it."

"You really think your mom is going to bust anytime soon?"

"Yeah, I am sure of it and my dad is home alone with her, I need to get home to check on him."

"Do you want me to come with you? It is four in the morning."

Steven thought about it, he did not want Mike to see his mom yet, especially if she is having an episode. He sat there for a couple of minutes and then an idea hit him.

"If you don't mind, can you ride halfway with me and I'll ride the other half? Our houses are only about a mile from each other which is about ten blocks, so how about you ride five there and I'll ride the other five, so this way we only have to ride halfway alone."

"You sure bro? I can come the whole way. I don't mind coming to your house with you." Steven thought about that, but even though Mike has heard all of the stories of his mom and dad, he did not want to have Mike see it in person.

"No, it's okay, just halfway, okay?"

Mike understood but did not tell Steven he knew he did not want him to see what could be happening at his house, he wanted to be supportive of Steven.

"Okay, let's get our bikes and go."

Steven and Mike left at 04:30, in the morning. It was still dark out, but the shifting of the temperature brings a smell in the air that Steven enjoyed this time of night. When the sun is slowly creeping up from the horizon where it is not just quite visible, the temperature brought with it the shifting winds that carried what Steven would call the morning smells—the smell of wet dew forming and the soil warming up, releasing its sweet smell of hidden life, under the dirt. It was springtime and flowers were slowly blooming and poking through the rich damp soil, from the April showers that pounded the Kansas land all the month of April. The smell of life was all around him, and it was the annual arrival of springtime. Steven felt that this was an odd resemblance of what was happening to him, an annual or semi-annual arrival of his mother's episode.

The moon's half-light illuminated the way for Steven and Mike. They lived in the part of town where it was far enough away from the city that streetlamps were only on every corner, not spread out fifty or so feet from each other. They reached the halfway point and they both stopped and looked at each other.

"You sure you don't want me to go the rest of the way with you?" Mike rolled his bike closer to Steven, his silver Mongoose reflected from the corner streetlight.

"No, I will be fine, I only have five blocks to go. Thanks Bro, I appreciate it."

"Okay, call me if you need anything, okay?"

"Okay."

They did give each other a half hug and Mike left. Steven stayed there to make sure Mike was really going home after he saw Mike's shadow roll past the next streetlamp, Steven turned around and rode for home.

Even though it was only five blocks to his house, Steven deep down hated the night when he was by himself. He enjoyed sleeping in the darkness, but he is in a room in a bed and is inside a house. However, walking about or riding his bike at night really scared him. He was always worried there was something lurking around the corner. Topeka is not the safest city, and with how much news his dad watches, he always heard about what happened in Topeka, especially at night.

He noticed he only had two blocks left and he heard a loud shriek coming from between houses. Steven's heart started to pound, and he could hear the blood circulating in his ears. He started to paddle faster; he figured he is on a bike and whatever it is, it is more likely on foot and he can outrun them with his bike. Suddenly, a black shadow came out from the house behind him and his blood froze.

"Oh man, what is that" The shadow began to grow bigger and started to move faster and towards Steven. He turned around and sped off as fast as he could. He could hear the footsteps grow louder and faster behind him and he did not want to look back; they were gaining on him and he peddled faster and then his pant leg got caught in the crank of his bike. He flipped over his handlebars and crashed straight on his stomach. He rolled over and saw the shadow running full force towards him, Steven closed his eyes and placed his arms over his face and looked away, prepared for the attack.

Suddenly his face was washed with warm wetness and the smell of saliva hit his nose. He opened his eyes to a large Pit Bull licking his face and wagging his tail.

"Oh my God, Brutus, it is just you. You damn dog, you scared the shit out of me."

Steven was laughing and began to pet Brutus. Brutus's name really did suite him well. He was a large Pit Bull weighing over eighty pounds. He was not fat by any means, but he had such powerful muscles and legs Steven was not surprised he had mistaken him for a person coming after him. Brutus kept licking Steven and put his full weight on him. Steven noticed that his shin was pretty scraped up from the crank shaft and Brutus smelled the blood and began to lick it.

"Stop it, Brutus, that stings." Steven took his pant leg out of the crank and turned around towards the closest streetlamp to get a better look at his leg. He saw that it was not that bad and the spikes from the crank scrapped across his leg only enough to draw blood but not so bad that it made a deep gash. He got up and walked around a bit while Brutus jumped up and down wanting to play.

"I'm sorry, boy, you need to get back home." Brutus perked his ears up when he heard the word "home" and sat down. "I'll walk you home and put you back in your yard. Next time, try not to escape again, okay?" Steven grabbed Brutus by his collar and walked him back home. Despite his scrapped leg he was sort of happy for this small diversion, then reality set in. "I need to get home." He then grabbed his bike and rode the last two blocks.

Steven rolled up to his house and checked his watch. It read 05:40 and he saw that the lights were on in his parent's bedroom and so were the living room and kitchen. His dad always got up at six, but he never put the bedroom light on. The living room and kitchen light were not what Steven thought odd, it was his parent's bedroom that worried him. He walked his bike to the porch and put the lock on it then walked up the porch, then he heard screaming coming from the house.

"Elaine open the damn door now!" Steven could hear his dad yelling from the living room. Steven ran into the living room and saw his dad trying to open the bedroom door. His dad was drenched in sweat and he had on some shorts and no shirt on. Joe saw Steven walk through the door.

"Steven, what are you doing here?"

"I had a weird feeling that something may have been wrong."

"What? Steven, I told you if you ever think your mom is going to have another episode, you are supposed to tell me immediately."

Joe looked mad and Steven could tell his dad had already been drinking this morning.

"I am sorry, I honestly did not think so at first," Steven flinched when his dad yelled at him.

"What the hell do you mean? If you suspected it, why didn't you tell me?"

Steven was getting mad, "It's because at first, I didn't think there was anything wrong; it wasn't until tonight I realized something was up!"

Joe was about to say something when Steven heard his mom screaming from the other side of the door.

"I will have you arrested! I am the Sherriff of Hartsorne County and I will take you back there!"

Steven thought about what she said, "Hartsorne," his mom was from Oklahoma, why is she saying she is the sheriff there?

"Did she say she is the Sheriff of Hartsorne?" Joe looked at Steven.

"Yeah, this is what she has been doing since midnight. She locked herself up in the room and keeps telling me she is a sheriff."

"What happened?"

"I don't know, she just snapped. I was up watching TV and she came out of the bedroom dressed in a sheriff costume and then began screaming at me. She had plastic handcuffs and tried to cuff me. I grabbed her then led her back into her room. I sat her down and tried to talk to her but then she attacked me and threw me out of the room and locked herself in."

Steven thought to himself and then walked over to his dad. "Dad let me see if she will let me talk to her."

Joe stepped away from the door, he was willing to try anything at this point. Usually, Joe would not let Steven get near his mother when she was like this, but he was desperate.

"Mom, it's me, Steven, can you open the door." Steven held his ear to the door and heard some shuffling from the other side. The door opened a crack and he saw that his dad was not lying. His mom was dressed in a sheriff uniform, but when he looked closer, he noticed it was not a real one; it was a costume from a party store. Steven could see his mom's face and her eyes looked empty. He could tell she was not there. He remembered that stare, that soulless stare; the last time he saw that was when she stared at him while holding the Mother Mary statue and chanting.

"I am the Sheriff of Hartsorne county, and that man Joseph Thomas is under arrest!" She held up a fake badge.

"Look, see my badge!" then she shut the door in Steven's face. It was quiet. Steven looked at his dad.

"We might have to do what we did last time."

"We can't, Joe said while drinking the beer he had laying

on the coffee table."

"Why?"

"Because it is Saturday."

Steven forgot it was only Saturday and she only goes to CARE on Monday, Wednesday, and Fridays. "So, we are stuck with her like this for two days?"

"Hell no," Joe said, crunching the beer can and throwing it in the trash can next to the couch.

"Well, what are we going to do?"

"I don't know, we might have to call a cab or something."

"I don't think that would be a good idea." Joe looked at Steven.

"Well, do you have an idea?"

"I think so . . ." Then Steven heard his mom began to yell again.

"Joseph Thomas you are under arrest!"

Steven saw his mom come out from the bedroom and there was something silver in her hand. Joe saw it too. "Steven, run into the kitchen now!" Steven saw his mom bring up the gun in both hands and aim it at his father. Steven ran to the kitchen and grabbed the phone to call the police. He heard a click noise and dropped the phone.

"Dad!"

Steven ran into the room and saw Joe tackle Elaine at the waist and they fell. He took the gun and threw it to the side. Steven picked it up and then dropped it, it was real! But it was not loaded.

"Steven, call the cops!"

"I was going to, but I thought she was going to shoot, I

heard a clicking noise and ran out here."

"Don't worry, it is not loaded, besides, the gun does not work anyways, she does not know that, but at this point I don't know what she may try to do."

Steven knew this was serious, his dad did not want the cops involved anymore, but for him to say to call, Steven knew it was serious. He could hear his mother screaming at the top of her lungs.

"Let me go, let me go! I am going to get backup soon! I already called!"

"What?" Joe yelled. "You already called?"

"Yeah, they will be here soon. You will be under arrest Joe Thomas!"

Steven picked up the phone from the floor and called, but when he put the phone to his ear, he could tell the line was dead.

"Dad, the phone is not working!"

"Seriously? Try the one in her bedroom, supposedly she called."

"Well, if she did, then should I still call?" He could hear his dad struggling against his mom.

"Yeah," Joe said while still barely holding on to Elaine. "Tell them that we are the ones that need help!"

Steven ran to the bedroom. When he got to the bedroom, he noticed that his suspicions were correct, he saw a plastic pack, from a party supply store, but his dad said the gun was real and Steven did not want to take a chance. He picked up the phone, but that line was dead, too.

"Dad, this one does not work either."

"Really?"

Elaine pushed Joe off; he fell on his back. Elaine got up and tried running towards the door.

"Backup is here!" Steven did not hear anything, but he ran towards his mom and grabbed her by the arm.

"Mom, stop! It's me, Steven!" Elaine turned around and looked at Steven in the eyes, but she was not there; no, it was someone completely different.

"I told you, I am a sheriff, unhand me or you will be under arrest too!" She pushed Steven back and he was twisted around from his mom and pushed forward, his injured leg hit the corner of the table and a sharp pain shot across his shin; he fell to the ground in pain.

Joe gathered his senses and ran to grab Elaine once again; this time, he grabbed her in a bear hug and looked at Steven.

"Steven, are you okay?" Steven was dazed, the pain was intense in his leg; he looked at it and saw that it was bleeding again. It was bruised and he didn't know if it was from earlier, now, or a combination of both, but his scrape was bruised black and blue and he saw that the cut was bigger now. After a minute, he finally returned to reality and heard his dad yelling at him.

"Steven, go across the street and get Cathy and Kent."

Steven got up and noticed the pain was easing up; it still hurt to walk on, but not as bad as after he hit it on the corner of the coffee table. Joe was slowly gaining ground on Elaine. He was able to drag her away from the door. Eventually, Joe got her back into the bedroom and closed the door. He knew it locked on the other side, but he was able to put enough hold

Episodes

on the door to keep Elaine from opening it.

"Steven, hurry up I don't know how much longer I can hold her."

Steven looked at his dad and then left. As Steven walked across the porch, he saw some garden sheers laying on the edge. He picked them up and looked at them. He then looked at the corner of the house and walked over to it. He saw the phone line running down the corning. Steven walked up closer to the phone line and saw that it was cut in half.

Now it makes sense why the phones are dead. He dropped the sheers on the ground and ran over towards Cathy and Kent's.

Steven knocked on the door with a rapid tap. He saw that the lights were on in the kitchen and then the living room light flicked on. Kent opened the door. He was Cathy's new boyfriend that she has been seeing for a couple of years. Zack mentioned it only a little bit. Zack did not hate the guy but did not like him; he only put up with him because his mom loved him. Kent was nice, but he was not Zack's real dad and Zack had always been like that to whoever Cathy dated. Kent was standing there with his work clothes on, he was an electrician and was tall and slender, he countered Cathy's heavyset frame.

"Steven, what's wrong?"

Steven was breathing heavy.

"It's my mom; my dad and I need help." Kent did not know much about Elaine's past but Cathy did and Cathy was standing behind Kent and heard Steven.

"Don't worry, Steven, we will come help." Cathy walked past Kent and told him to come. He didn't say a word and followed. Cathy, Kent, and Steven walked into the house and saw Joe desperately holding on to the door. Kent and Cathy heard Elaine yelling from behind the door. Steven told Cathy everything that happened. Cathy looked at Steven and Joe. "Cathy," Joe said panting, drenched in sweat again, fighting hard to keep the door from opening.

"We do not have much time and I really don't want the cops involved; earlier I did, but now I have a plan."

"What is it?" Cathy looked at Joe, listening. Kent just stood there shocked at what was going on.

"Why don't we call the cops; we can use our phone."

"No, Kent, we can do this." Steven was shocked to hear Cathy saying it, he thought she would be all for it.

"What is your plan, Joe?"

"Well, she keeps saying that she called for backup, but Steven said the phones are dead."

"Yeah, he told us the line was cut." Joe looked at Cathy in surprise, he did not know that since Steven found it after he told him to get them.

"I figured," Joe mumbled to himself. "Anyways, since she thinks she has backup coming, you two can act like you are the backup."

"What if she doesn't think so?" Kent said with a twinge in his voice.

"Well, it is a gamble we need to take." Cathy said looking at Kent.

"Okay, I guess, what the hell." Kent threw up his hands in the air.

"Okay Joe, let me and Kent come up to the door."

"Have at it." Then Joe let go of the door. "Elaine, this is officer S and K." Elaine went quiet. Steven and Joe looked at each other.

Elaine slowly opened the door and saw Kent and Cathy standing there. Steven and Joe began to think that Elaine was not going to buy it and remember them.

"Thank God you two are here, that man is under arrest!" Cathy and Kent looked at each other then looked back at Elaine.

"Yes," Cathy cut in before Kent was going to say something.

"Let's take them to the courthouse together."

"Okay."

Elaine walked out and brought cuffs, Steven could tell they were just plastic cuffs from the party store but Joe played along and turned around and placed his hands behind his back. Elaine put them on and walked with Cathy and Kent.

"We will take our van, we parked across the street."

"Okay, oh and bring that boy too, he is under arrest for attacking me earlier." Steven was going to go anyways, so he played along.

Cathy and Kent got Elaine into their van. Joe and Steven rode in the back. They headed to the hospital. Elaine realized where they were going.

"Officer S and K, why are we going here?"

"Because Joe was complaining of injuries, we have to get him checked out first.

"Oh, okay, protocol, good work."

When they arrived at the hospital, Steven stayed behind while his dad, Cathy and Kent walked Elaine into the hospital.

"Why is the boy not coming?" Elaine stared back at Steven in the van.

"Because he was not injured, we are only getting Joe checked out." Steven heard the conversation as they walked into the hospital; he thought how it was ironic the way it played out—he was the one injured but he did not want to go in. He stayed in the van, with tears running down his cheek, and looked away from the hospital.

EPISODE FIVE

Two months passed, since Elaine was admitted to the hospital. A couple weeks ago, she was transferred to a mental hospital ward that only deals with severe cases, of which Elaine has been numerous times. Joe and Steven were lucky and grateful for Cathy and Kent who helped bring Elaine to the hospital and played along with the rouse. Joe honestly did not think it would have worked at the time, but he had to give anything a try to get Elaine help without the police involved. He knew he took a gamble having Cathy help, because he did not know what she might do. To Joe's surprise and gratitude, nothing had happened during the two months Elaine had been away.

The last two months, Steven had been spending more nights at Mike's house even during school nights. Joe did not mind that Steven was staying at Mike's so much. In fact, Joe liked having the house to himself and not having to worry about Steven needing something to eat. Joe also liked having the home to himself so he could watch TV without interruption. He did not mind when he and Steven sometimes talked, but Joe secretly enjoyed the solitude and being able to watch his sports without worrying if Steven was going to pop out of his room. But the main reason Joe did not mind Steven spending so much time with Mike is because Joe could not remember Steven ever having a best friend besides Zack. Steven seemed to be in better spirits, even after this recent episode and Joe was pleased that Mike was there to help out Steven. Joe knew that Zack had moved on to high school life and his social gatherings has changed. He knew that Steven and Zack did not spend time with each other much now, if any. But Joe was happy Steven had someone to rely on besides himself. And he knew he was not always there for Steven emotionally, but at least Mike was.

Today was Friday and Joe knew that Steven would be spending the night at Mike's. But tomorrow, Joe was going to visit Elaine in the hospital. When Steven returns home, he was going to try to convince him to visit her tomorrow. Elaine had been asking for Steven to come by which is highly unusual for her. When she is in the mental ward, she still does not know much of anyone except Joe, at this point of her post-episode healing. Elaine usually did not ask for Steven, or anyone else, until she was at the stage of release into a functional, halfway house environment or when she was already at one. However, Joe was surprised when Elaine asked him. Joe sat there in silence waiting for Steven to come home; he knew it would only be ten minutes, so Joe grabbed a beer and put on the news and waited for Steven to arrive.

Joe heard Steven's bike brakes squeal in front of the porch. He turned off the TV. Joe really wanted Steven to know how important it was for him to visit his mother. He heard the door open and watched Steven go into his room and come back out with his things for the weekend.

"Hey, Steven."

"Hey, Dad, I'm going over to Mike's house, is it still okay?" Steven knew it was, but he always asked out of respect for his dad.

"Yeah, it is, but I have something to ask you." Joe finished his beer and crumpled the can.

"What's up?" Steven stopped at the door and looked at his dad. Steven was really curious about what his dad wanted; they had not talked much, since the last episode.

"Tomorrow, I am going to visit your mom . . ." and before Joe could finish, Steven jumped in.

"Okay, let me know how it goes." Steven was about to leave.

"Steven, I was not finished." Joe sounded a little angry.

"Sorry," Steven looked down.

"Anyways, your mom has asked to see you." Steven looked at his dad in surprise, his mom asked for him while still in the mental ward. He was never asked to come by his mom.

"I don't know, Dad . . . I . . ."

"It would mean the world to her, Steven."

Steven did not know what to do. His dad has asked him to go visit several times, but he never wanted to go. Steven was always afraid bad memories would stir when seeing her in that state. He never knew how she was at this stage in her healing, but he was always afraid she may relapse or still would be so far off that he felt it was pointless. But deep down, Steven did not want to see her in a mental ward. Steven had heard stories from people and watched too many movies depicting crazy people that were screaming and locked up in straitjackets. He never wanted to know if his mom was one of those and did not want to add another visual to his nightmares by seeing his mom like that.

"Dad, you know how I feel about going." Steven stood there by the door unmoving, toying with the idea slightly, then he shook his head without his dad seeing it. Steven made up his mind and did not want to go.

"Steven, I know how you feel and about what you think she may look like there, but she is not like that. She is at the point of being well enough to know who you are, and she has been able to list off family, friends, and neighbors. Honestly, I am surprised she has not been let out yet, she seems well enough."

"Well, can I just wait until she is in the functioning home first? If what you say is true, she should be in one in a couple of days. I promise I will visit her then."

"Steven, I said I am surprised she is not out yet, not that she will be out soon. Please, do this for your mom, she really has been asking to see you." Joe stood up and went to throw away the empty beer can and to grab a fresh one from the fridge. He knew it would be a little bit before Steven would reply.

Steven stood there and his heart was pounding; he was retracting the previous decision he had made up in his head and was actually toying with the idea of going to see his mom. He stood there for a moment and felt that his hand was slipping from the doorknob with sweat; the whole time he never took his hand off the cold, metal knob.

"Can I think about it over the night, Dad?" Joe stood there

staring into the fridge, he really wanted an answer now, but if Steven was really considering it, he did not want to push him.

"Okay, how about this, you please think about it and call me right at ten in the morning from Mike's house, okay? But I really want you to visit your mom, she has never asked for you before when she was in the hospital. Usually, she is still delusional and still playing out the episode, but she really does seem better, so please really think about it." Joe closed the fridge and walked towards Steven and looked him in the eyes not saying a word; he was hoping that maybe silently staring at him would help. Steven looked up at his dad and stood there quietly. Deep down he wanted to see his mom, but he was still having doubts.

"Okay, Dad, I promise I will truly consider it, just give me tonight to think about it, okay?"

Steven stood there staring back at his dad in silence, he could feel his heart still pounding and his anxiety was elevated; he just wanted to leave at this point.

"Okay," his dad finally breaking the awkward silence. "Call me at ten in the morning." Then Joe turned around and walked towards the couch. Steven watched his dad and made sure his dad had nothing else to say. Joe gave him a goodbye backhand wave while watching the news. Steven knew that it meant his dad was done talking, so he turned around and left.

"Hi, Miss. Adison, I am here to stay the night." Steven looked at Mike's mom who opened the door. She stood there, with her blonde hair and hazel eyes. Steven always found

Mike's mom really attractive but had never told him. Miss Adison has been nicer lately and Mike said it is because she decided to take a job at a different, larger firm where she is now the lead paralegal. Mike said his mom received a significant raise and now that she watches over several other paralegals, she does not get the brunt of the casework. She usually is the one that looks it over after the ones below her put together the information.

"Hello, Steven, how are you today?" Miss Adison had a happy gleam in her eye and Steven noticed that she was wearing perfume and that it was fresh. She was wearing a black cocktail dress and had on light, pink lipstick. Steven noticed she was wearing open-toed, high heels and had nail polish that matched her fingers—a light pink to accent her lipstick.

"I am doing okay I guess." Steven looked at her; she looked really nice and he could not stop staring at her.

"Hey Steven, I am in the bedroom, go ahead and come in," Steven heard Mike call from the back of the house.

"I'll see you later, Steven, I ordered pizza for you and Mike."

"Are you not going to eat?"

"No, I am going on a date tonight, but you two have fun, I'll be home before ten." Then she walked out of the house and left in her car.

"Hey, Mike, what's up?"

"Nothing, just doing some writing is all." Steven saw Mike hunched over a large note pad, with his blonde hair covering his face. He stopped writing and looked over at Steven.

"Everything okay?" Besides seeing how pretty Mike's mom was, Steven's mood was still sour from earlier; he did not want to tell Mike and wanted to deal with this on his own.

"Yeah, I'm okay. Anyways, your mom said she was going out on a date tonight, you all right?" Steven looked at Mike and was expecting him to either deny he was okay or say how much he hated the new guy his mom was seeing.

"Honestly, I am okay, Steven. My dad never comes around to visit anymore and the new person my mom is seeing is making her happy. Yeah, her new job has helped out a lot with her mood, but the new person she is seeing is making her happy enough so that she does not seem angry at the world anymore. I have my old mom back and I am happy for that, as long as she is happy, I am happy. I know that sounds so cliché, but seriously, if she is in a sour mood, she lays it on me, because I am the only one here. But now that she has someone else to unload onto, that keeps me happy, because she is not dealing out her frustration on me, which I understand. It is nice to have my mom back to her normal, happy self."

Steven could tell Mike was not lying. Mike in the past couple of weeks did seem to be happier. Also, his mom was a really good cook. Steven has noticed the atmosphere at Mike's house between him and his mom was much better. Despite Mike living in a single parent home, this was the closest to normality that Steven had ever felt.

This is why Steven has been staying the night more often at Mikes; he felt like he was part of a normal family. Mike and Steven were getting as close as brothers and Steven felt like he had been pseudo-adopted by Miss. Adison. She cooked some nights things Steven enjoyed, they watched movies together with her, and he went on errands with Mike and her sometimes. Steven, of course, enjoyed spending time with Mike and hanging around writing and playing video games, but these past two months, Steven felt he was part of a normal, functioning family. Also, all this time away from his own home has kept his mind off of his own situation and helped with his nightmares.

"Well, I am glad she is happy, because you do seem much happier these past several weeks." Steven laid out his sleeping bag and got out his own writing supplies from his backpack.

"Thanks, Steven, I appreciate it." Mike looked at Steven and gave him a big smile.

"Hey, is it okay if I do some writing right now, Mike? I know you have been doing some while I was at home getting my stuff."

"No, it's cool, go ahead, I am still needing to finish up."

After a half an hour passed, Mike and Steven heard the old doorbell ring. It was not hard to miss even with the doors closed; it produced such a high pitched "ding, ding, ding" sound that Steven thought the house behind them could hear. They both remembered and cried out "Pizza!" in unison. Mike gave the delivery guy the money and tip and brought in the sweet smell of melted cheese and marinara sauce covered pizza into his room. It was their favorite—straight cheese pizza with extra cheese and sauce. Mike opened it up and did the string test. He lifted up the first piece and saw the steam rising from the pizza and how the cheese was oozing from the piece he held up, with dozens of strings of cheese leading to the rest of the pie. "Ah, the best kind of pizza, so much cheese, it just oozes with golden brown strings glistening against the box."

Steven grabbed the paper plates and they began to devour the whole thing. Usually, Mike's mom shared between them but since she was not home tonight, they both ate half a pizza.

"Man, I am stuffed." Steven wiped away some of the sweet, sticky grease from his chin. "Yeah, this one was probably one of the best in a long time."

"Agreed." Steven closed his eyes, the smell of stale pizza crust still lingering in the air. "Hey, what do you want to do tonight? My mom is not home, and we could watch anything we want." Steven still had his eyes closed; he partially heard Mike but he was still thinking about possibly visiting his mother. The high of the pizza was wearing off and his conversation with his dad was replaying in his mind. "Steven, did you hear me?" Mike was staring at Steven intently.

"Yeah, yeah. Sorry, you said we could watch anything we want."

"Yeah, we should watch an extra violent movie or something."

"Yeah, what do you have in mind?"

"I don't know really, I never really watched anything too gory, since my mom won't let me."

Steven did not know either. His parents did not have the large, cable package that Mike's house did. Steven's dad paid for the lowest tier which still had about fifty channels, half of them sports and news, but he still got the most popular channels that most everyone had. Mike on the other hand had the ultimate package that included every channel that COX offered, and included HBO, Cinemax, and STARZ. Mike's mom would only let them watch certain movies and even if they watched them in Mike's room, she had a habit of just popping in unannounced. Plus, they usually just played games or wrote so they never were really tempted to watch anything anyway.

"I don't know, whatever really, how about we just flip the channels, until we see the bloodiest, curse word filled, least amount of clothes thing we can find." Steven had a grin on his face trying to hide what he was really thinking about.

"Okay, that sounds like a plan." They went into the living room and turned on the TV until Mike found a movie they did not know, but it was everything they ever wanted. On the TV, there was a woman running in the street, with blood running down her left side of her body. Her light, brown hair was covered in blood and dirt and she was limping while running. Her top was off, and she was only wearing tattered jeans that were just as dirty as the rest of her.

"Wow" they both said in unison.

"I've never seen a girl topless before," Mike said moving closer to the TV. Steven blushed and looked down. That is one thing he had never told Mike—that he has seen a woman topless before, but it was of his mother, during one of her episodes.

"Yeah, me neither," Steven softly said only loud enough that Mike could barely hear. They finished watching the movie in silence and when it was over, they realized it was getting close to nine.

"Well, my mom will be home soon, want to go to my room and play some video games, until we crash?"

"Yeah, that sounds fine."

Steven was still thinking about what he and his father talked about and the rest of the night Steven did not talk. Mike knew the whole time that there was something bothering Steven ever since he first came over, but he thought Steven would have told him what was wrong by now.

"Steven, I know something is wrong, what is it?"

"There is nothing wrong."

"Bro, don't bullshit me; we are as close as brothers and by now, I know there is something wrong. You know I won't leave you alone until you tell me." Steven knew Mike was right, he would nag him until he caved, so instead of just denying it for an hour or two and dragging it out until he caves, which he always does, he told Mike everything he and his father talked about.

Mike sat there silently then told Steven what he didn't want to hear.

"Honestly, your dad is right, you need to go see your mom."

"I was hoping you wouldn't say that." Steven looked down at his controller in his hands and then set it down and laid back on his sleeping bag, covering his face with both hands.

"Why? You even said yourself you were considering going." Mike began to stare at Steven like Joe did earlier, Steven could feel Mike's gaze on him even with his hands over his eyes.

"Yeah, but if you told me I shouldn't, I would not go, but since you are saying yes, now I really have to consider it."

"Consider it?" Mike raised his voice not in anger, but in surprise.

"No, you are going to do it. What could it hurt? If what you think happens is true, then you never will have to go again."

"But if it is true, then I will probably have nightmares again."

"But what if it is not true, what if this whole time you ignored visiting your mom and it's not as bad as you say, huh?" Steven closed his eyes and breathed in. He knew Mike was right.

"Besides, you said your mom never asked until today, now she wants you to—you can at least give her that. I know you have some issues with her, but you said when she is sane, she is really sweet. The few times I have met her, she reminds me of my mom." Steven rolled over and stared at Mike; he has never heard anyone compare his mom to someone else who is normal.

"Really?"

"Yeah, you said so yourself, you said your mom is really cool and stuff when she is not sick. Plus, the few meals I've had at your place when she has cooked are really good." Steven looked at Mike and smiled. He has never heard anyone compliment his mom and compare her to their own mother. Every other person made fun of his mother or reminded him how his mom is different.

"Can I use your phone?"

"Sure, what for?"

"I'm going to call my dad and let him know I am going." Steven dialed his number and saw it was eleven p.m., he knew his dad would still be up. "Hello" Steven heard his dad answer in a questionable tone; he didn't blame him, not many people call this late at night.

"It's me, Dad. I decided I will go with you tomorrow." Joe

closed his eyes and smiled.

"Good choice, Steven, I am proud of you. I will see you when you get home tomorrow."

Steven hung up the phone and smiled.

"What's up?" Mike asked wondering what was going through Steven's mind.

"My dad said he was proud of me."

Steven arrived home at noon and Joe was watching a baseball game on TV.

"Hey, Dad, I'm home, we going to visit mom still?"

Joe turned around and saw Steven walk through the door. He was happy that Steven agreed to go to the hospital to visit Elaine.

"Yes, we will leave now, if you are ready." Joe turned off the TV and walked to the kitchen to get the keys to his Dodge.

"Yeah, now sounds good." Steven's heart was slowly beginning to pound faster and harder. Through the night, he stayed up playing out what will happen at the hospital and his fears kept him up.

Steven played out the best scenarios over and over in his mind to help him get ready to visit his mom, but now that the hour was here, no matter how many times he played the best-case scenes in his mind, the realization of going to visit his mother in the mental hospital leapt into his mind. Now all he was thinking about was screaming people in straitjackets, and his mom a part of it all and his worst fear—she herself is the one in the jacket screaming. Steven shook his head and realized his dad was halfway to the truck.

"You coming, Steven?" Joe had his large 44oz jug that Steven knew was half whiskey and water.

"Yeah, I am ready."

The hospital was a forty-minute drive from their house; it was situated in a small, unincorporated town west of Kansas City. When Joe parked, Steven saw the large letters above the entrance that read "STATE BEHAVIORAL HEALTH HOSPITAL" but Steven knew that it was a nice way of saying a mental hospital. Steven and Joe walked in and the way that Steven imagined it would look was true. The reception desk stood about fifty feet from the entrance and Steven saw that the first floor was completely white. The reception desk was white, with a light gray countertop. The floors had white tile with little black specks that were dotted like tiny, little stars, with no order or arrangement. There were doors lined evenly on each side of the first floor. Light gray doors that Steven noticed were made out of metal and not wood. The windows of the doors were small and rectangular and he saw that there was honeycombed, metal mesh inside each window. Then there was the smell. Steven has been in a regular hospital before and there was always that smell that he would describe as sterile—a mix of alcohol and other cleaning solutions he was sure was only used at a hospital. Here, it smelled heavily of cleaning solution he had never smelled before; it smelled so chemically to him he could hardly inhale it with his nose. He tried to breathe with his mouth open, but the smell was so strong he could taste it. Steven gave up and let the chemical cleaning solution assault his taste and smell.

Steven and Joe walked up to the receptionist. She was wearing a white uniform and white shoes. The only thing that had color besides her dark brown hair and hazel brown eyes was the black leather belt she wore around her dress. He noticed it looked more like a designer belt to help give some flair to an otherwise bland and boring uniform. "Hello, may I help you?" She looked up and smiled at Joe and looked over at Steven.

"Oh, hello, Joseph, is this your son?" Joe smiled back.

"Yes, this is Steven, he is here to visit his mother, Elaine."

"Oh, how sweet, your mother has been wanting to see you the past couple of weeks; it is very sweet of you to come visit your mother." Steven didn't reply, he simply nodded. "Not much of a talker, are you?" The receptionist chuckled and smiled. "Anyways, she's still in room 303 on the top floor."

"Okay, thank you." Joe grabbed two visitor badges and they walked over to the elevator. To Steven's surprise, the elevator had a wood grain interior and lights that were not as bright as the intense white that filled the first floor.

Joe and Steven arrived on the top floor and stepped out. Steven was not surprised to see that the top floor looked just like the first, it was just as white and smelled just as pungent to him as the first. The setup was the same too, there was a receptionist desk in the middle, with rows of metal doors lining each side of the room. Joe walked up to the lady who was just like the one downstairs and wore the same uniform.

"You must be Joe."

She had strawberry blonde hair with some white hairs woven in. She looked to be in her early fifties but still had very fair and soft looking skin. Her blue eyes sparkled against the white lighting from the ceiling and then she looked over towards Steven.

"Hello, are you Elaine's son? She has talked much about you." Steven just nodded. "I am your mother's nurse. My name is Julie Silva but many people around here just call me 'Silv' for short."

She got up to shake Steven's hand and he saw that she was very short; she was not much taller than Steven and he was hitting just under five feet. Steven never had anyone offer their hand to him before but he had seen many people shake hands, so he slowly hung his hand out and let her do the shaking.

"Well, it is nice to meet you; if you two are ready, she is waiting to see you both." Steven and Joe walked with nurse Silv, and along the way, Steven noticed that it was not as bad as he had imagined. The interior of the building was what he had imagined, but everything else was not as bad. There were no screaming or random people running around in straitjackets. What he sensed was a feeling of calmness. When walking passed the doors, he would briefly peek into the doors to see the people inside, most were sleeping, some were watching the small TVs provided in the rooms. When he got to the next to last door, something caught his eye.

Steven saw a man sitting on top of his bed. He was bald and his head looked red but Steven could not tell for sure. Steven could see the man rocking back and forth but he did not say anything. He then saw that the man began to talk, so he placed his ears against the cold steel door and heard nothing. He moved his ear onto the glass and still did not hear anything, either the glass was too thick or the man was just lipping the words and not saying anything. When Steven pulled his ear away from the window, he saw that the man's hair was laying all over the floor. In amazement, Steven looked back at the man's head and saw that it was red with blood and that his hands were covered in it as well. Steven stepped back in shock. Silv walked up to Steven and said, "Come on, honey, your mom is waiting for you." Steven just stood there staring into the room; he could not take his eyes off of what he saw.

"Steven, what's wrong?" Steven stood their silently. Silv stepped in front of him and looked into the door.

"Oh God! Dr. Hutchinson, we need you to room 301 now!" Silv gently guided Steven by the hand towards Joe. "Here Joe, take Steven to see Elaine, you two can go in now, I have an emergency to take care of." Steven just stood there in silence, replaying what he saw in his mind.

Steven and Joe walked into Elaine's room. It was lit by the natural sunlight filtering into the room. Elaine was lying in her bed watching TV. When Steven and Joe walked in, she turned off the TV and looked towards them. She was smiling and the sun illuminated her wet hair.

"Hey, you guys made it just in time, I just got done taking a shower a couple of minutes ago. I thought you would come a little bit later."

"Yeah, I decided to come a little bit earlier, since Steven came home early from Mike's today."

Joe grabbed a chair and sat by Elaine. Steven looked for somewhere to sit and saw a windowsill that was large enough to fit two people and sat. The sun's rays coming through the windows felt warm to him and he enjoyed it; the warming embrace helped ease some of what he witnessed earlier. Steven was getting used to seeing obscure things in his life because of his mom and in ways was growing numb to it, but they would usually catch up to him in the form of horrible nightmares. He knew what he just witnessed would be something that he will face at night. He shook his head and tried to focus on his mother.

"Steven," Elaine turned her head towards him smiling. "I am so happy you came to visit your mother."

She held out her hands, gesturing that she wanted a hug. Steven deep down loved his mother, but he did not like physical touching much. He guessed he was never hugged enough to get used to it, but he went over to give his mom a hug. It was an awkward hug for Steven, especially since Elaine was lying down in bed, but Steven did not know how to really hug her back, so he just laid one arm over her and accepted her two arms while using only one of his and using the other to balance himself.

"Oh, how I missed you!" Elaine said out loud.

Steven noticed there was a very faint smell he had never really noticed before; he did not know if it was some sort of special soap the facility used but it smelled faint and very unique. Steven swore he had smelled it before but could not figure out what it was. After the hug, Steven walked back to the window and sat there quietly.

"I've got good news!" Elaine sat up higher in her bed. "The doctor said that I am doing so well that I can come home today, isn't that great?"

"Really?" Joe said a little confused. "That is really quick, don't they usually put you in a functioning home first, until you can finally come home?"

"Yeah, but the doctor said that I am well enough to skip that."

Steven sat there, he always wanted to know for sure if his mother ever knew why she was there. Did she know about her episodes or did she think it was something else.

"Well, I brought the truck, so it will be a little cramped."

"That's okay, Steven can sit in the middle; he is skinny enough to fit." Elaine chuckled looking at Steven.

"Okay, as long as you think we can fit in a single seat cab truck, we will have to put your stuff in the bed then."

"That's okay," Elaine got up and began grabbing her things. Steven realized nothing was going to lead to what he wanted to know, so he finally spoke for once, since arriving at the hospital.

"So, Mom, are you feeling okay?" He looked at her while she was packing. She was already dressed in her normal clothes; he saw that the hospital gown was under her blankets on the bed.

"I feel great, Steven, like I said, the doctor said I am good to go home."

Steven did not know what to say next, he wanted to ask without asking *do you remember your episodes?* So, he thought of a different route.

"Mom, dad was the one who dropped you off when you were sick; he forgot to tell me why you were here." Joe looked at Steven with a glare.

"Oh, just the usual reason, my depression was very high is all."

So, there it is; she thinks it is just her depression. He wanted to know if she could recall her episodes, but Joe interrupted.

"Steven get your mom's stuff and take it to the truck." Steven looked at his dad and could tell he was angry with him.

"Okay," is all Steven said. He grabbed his mom's bags and took them to the truck. As Steven walked past the bathroom, he smelled that weird smell again, just as faint and familiar as before. He wanted to go in, but his dad kept egging him on.

"Come on Steven, hurry up while I check out your mother. We will be down shortly."

Steven did not fight his dad; he did what his dad told him. As Steven was walking out, he saw the man from earlier being sent away in an ambulance.

Elaine had been back home for over a week. Steven felt that things might get back to normal, or at least to what was normal for his home. His mom had been in a cleaning mood ever since she had come back from the hospital. Joe seemed to enjoy coming home to an extra clean house after work. Elaine would get up and clean the whole house every day. She would first take a shower, get dressed and make breakfast for Steven. Joe asked Steven not to spend the nights over at Mike's house as often, so Elaine would not feel like he did not want to be around her. Steven could still go on Friday nights and Steven said it was okay.

After Steven went to school, Elaine would then start

cleaning the house. The next day after her release, she cleaned out the garage behind the house. That following Monday, she cleaned the shed and then the rest of the week, she went to each room doing a deep clean. Steven did not pay much attention and didn't think anything odd about it. He knew excessive cleanings were sometimes her first tell when she was getting sick. But first, Steven had never seen her become sick immediately after she arrived home; it was usually several months out. Usually, when she is like that, she is still in the medical system having relapses, before finally coming home. Plus, the two times she had cleaning episodes, she was putting things in bags and placing everything in the living room. However, she was cleaning in a way Steven had always imagined normal cleaning to be. She would dust, vacuum, mop, clean counters, and etc. If she put things in bags, it was a small amount and she was throwing it away immediately, not stuffing the bags and putting them in the living room as before.

The only thing that really stood out to Steven was that smell he detected on his mother the day they brought her back. Ever since she had been home, he noticed that the house smelled like that odor, but it was very faint, almost fainter than on her. Steven did not know if it was soap that she may have been using that was left over from the hospital, and it was wafting throughout the house, or maybe it was something she was cleaning with. He could not tell for sure.

Steven came home from school and everything was normal for his home. His mom was making dinner when he arrived, and she would tell him what she was making. Today, they were going to eat baked chicken, green beans, and corn. Steven then went to his room and waited until his dad came home and then they had dinner in the living room. Joe put on the news and his mom and dad ate on the couch, one on each end, and Steven ate on the brown recliner adjacent to his parents. After they were done eating, Elaine took their dishes and began to clean up the kitchen. Steven went to his room while his dad drank beer and watched TV, until he went to sleep. The rest of the night went as usual.

Steven stayed up till about midnight and decided it was finally time to go to bed. He heard the TV in his parent's room. He figured his mom was probably still watching TV while his dad was sleeping. So, Steven went to bed and laid there fighting sleep, until he would finally pass out an hour later. Then he woke up to an intense smell; he rolled over to check his clock and saw that it was three in the morning. The smell was intense and assaulting to his nose; it was also burning his eyes. He got up in bed and when he yawned and inhaled through his nose, it stung intensely. *What is this?* he thought to himself. He walked closer to his bedroom door and the smell was getting stronger, not only that, but now it was beginning to burn his nose.

Steven opened his bedroom door and felt like he walked into an invisible wall. The smell was intense, and his eyes began to burn even more. His eyes began to water, and he could not breathe without his throat burning. He took his shirt and held it over his mouth and nose, so the burning would be less intense. Steven looked into his parent's bedroom and saw that they were both out of bed. He walked into the living room and saw that the living room was dark. Steven saw light coming at the end of the house where the bathroom was. He could hear his dad whispering. Steven could not hear what was going on, but he knew his parents must be in the bathroom. He wanted to know what was happening. As he approached closer to the bathroom, he could feel a heavier presence engulfing him. The smell felt physical now, not only was the smell increasing and the burning getting worse, but even with his shirt covering his mouth and nose—the air just felt warm and heavy. Whatever was causing the smell was changing the feel of the air around him.

Steven got to the small hallway between the living room and bathroom. Steven saw his dad blocking the doorway talking quietly. The smell was coming from the bathroom and it was so intense, Steven did not know how his dad was able to stand so close to it. When Steven got closer, he could tell it was affecting his dad, because Joe's voice sounded raspy and in pain.

"Elaine, what the hell are you doing? I told you to stop." Steven could barely hear his mom. He wanted to get closer, but the smell was like a physical barrier; this was as far as Steven could go. Joe saw Steven's reflection from the bathroom mirror.

"Damn it, Elaine, you woke up Steven." Joe turned around and turned on the hallway light. When the light came on, Steven could see that his dad's eyes were red and watery. Steven could tell it was not due to crying, but whatever was causing the smell was burning his dad's eyes too.

"Steven, go back to bed." Joe's voice was raised to normal

talking level, but his voice sounded even more raspy.

"What's going on, Dad?"

"Nothing, just go back to bed." Joe stepped towards Steven, but Steven ran past him. Steven broke through the intense wall of smell and there was his mother on her hands and knees, with nothing but a bra and underwear on.

"What the hell?" Steven gasped, and it was a very painful gasp. He inhaled sharply from the pain and the inhale made it even worse. Steven saw what was causing the smell throughout the house and saw dozens of empty bleach bottles all over the bathroom floor. Steven saw that the bath was filled halfway with bleach and based on how strong it was, it was not diluted. Elaine stayed on her hands and knees ignoring Steven. She was talking to herself and Steven saw that she was wet, and her skin was bright red. His mom then dumped a bottle of bleach on the tile floor repeating, "I must clean away all of my sins." She was repeating this the whole time Steven was standing there in shock. His mom seemed so calm and was unaware of the world around her. Joe came up to Steven.

"She has been doing this the past hour or so." Steven looked at his dad. "When I found her, she was dumping bleach on herself." Steven looked at his mom. He saw that it was not sweat on his mom, but it was bleach. She took the rag she was using and then wrung it out over herself still saying, "I must clean away all of my sins."

"What are we going to do? It is Tuesday morning and she does not have CARE today." Steven began walking back towards the living room; the intense smell of bleach was taking its toll.

"I don't know, I tried talking to her, but she just kept

ignoring me." Joe began to open the windows in the living room to air out the house. The cool March air began to come into the house and Steven ran next to the window to inhale the sweet fresh air.

"Maybe we just ignore her for a couple of hours." Steven looked at his dad thinking that he would think it was a stupid idea. Joe looked at his son.

"At this point, I am willing to try anything." Joe walked next to Steven and began to inhale the air coming from the window as well. After about ten minutes passed, Steven heard the tub drain. "You hear that?" Joe pulled away from the window and heard it too.

"Yeah, it sounds like the bathtub draining."

"I hope it is, maybe that will help with this intense smell."

"Yeah, I hope so. I really wanted to go outside but I knew that standing on the porch at almost four in the morning would look weird to the neighbors."

"Especially, if both of us were." Steven chimed in.

As quickly as it started, it ended just as fast. Elaine emerged out of the bathroom and then went to the bedroom. Joe went to the bathroom and saw that the tub was empty. The smell was still strong, since there was bleach on the floor. He opened the window, turned off the light, and closed the door. It was not immediate relief, but it was enough that the house was starting to become easier to breathe in. Steven walked to his parent's door and saw that his mom was sleeping, still with just her bra and underwear.

"Dad, should I stay up tonight?" Steven looked at his dad. Joe was downing a beer.

"No, go back to bed, I'll stay up just in case."

"Okay." Steven did not want to be in the living room, it still smelled of bleach. He figured since his room was the farthest from the bathroom, it would be better in there. When he entered his room, he noticed there was still a lingering smell of bleach, but it was just a smell at this point and not so intense that it affected his eyes or nose. He knew he would not be able to sleep tonight, so he just turned on a reading light and began to write. He felt that writing would be the only thing to help him feel better.

When the sun rose, Elaine got up. Steven heard his mother stirring in the bedroom and heard her go into the living room. Steven stepped out and saw that his dad was still up watching TV. Elaine stepped up to Joe and asked him if he wanted breakfast. Joe looked up at her.

"Do you remember anything from last night Elaine?" She just looked at him. "Elaine?" She just stood there.

"Elaine, I think you may need to go back to the hospital, I don't think you are all the way better." Elaine started to sob and cried out.

"Yes, yes, I need help!" She then fell down crying. Steven closed his door. He could hear his dad getting the car keys and heard his mom and dad leave. This was the first time his mom ever left willingly.

EPISODE SIX

After the last episode, it was determined that Elaine was not completely well when she came out of the hospital in the first place. When Elaine went in after her bleaching episode, Joe talked with the doctors and found out that she was hiding her illness during the psychology evaluations. The week leading up to Elaine being released from the hospital, she was able to trick the doctors into believing that she was well. Elaine was telling the evaluators what they wanted to hear so she could get out of the hospital. She did a very good job at hiding it because she fooled Joe for a week, until the night when she poured bleach over herself. Steven had a gut feeling something was odd when she was home, but he had to admit this episode came out of nowhere. He had to think of the circumstances leading up to it, the fact that she was released from the behavioral rehabilitation hospital and not from a functioning home was a sign, but the constant cleaning was different this time. She still cooked dinner, watched her shows, and cleaned, but in the end, it still fooled both Steven and Joe.

Elaine was released from a functioning home six months

later, and everything was normal again or what could be normal for Steven. Except Joe had been drinking heavily the past six months, because when Elaine was released, Joe's brother, Christopher, was diagnosed with cirrhosis of the liver. Joe took it badly and had been on edge with Elaine and Steven. Joe usually had a temper, but the littlest of things provoked him such as walking in front of the TV when a sports game was on or even if someone flushed the toilet with the door open.

Steven had never met Uncle Christopher but his dad told him stories about growing up in New York together. They were very close when growing up. Joe told Steven that they once even owned a business together in New York but when it failed, they decided to move out to the west coast and open a deli there too. When that one failed, Christopher met a woman and moved to Arizona. Joe moved to Oklahoma for a job, met Elaine and moved to Kansas. Joe never talked much about his past life to Steven, but he did hear many of the stories of the things his father and uncle did together when growing up.

Steven talked to his uncle a couple of times, but he was always drunk over the phone. Uncle Chris was a happy drunk but when Steven would try to talk to him, he was so out of it and happy, his sentences made no sense. So, whenever he heard his dad talking to Uncle Chris, he would just keep walking so his dad would not ask if he wanted to talk to him. Steven did feel bad for his uncle having been diagnosed with a horrible disease, but he was not as close to him as he was to Uncle Terry.

One Sunday morning when Steven got out of bed to go

to the restroom, he heard his dad in the kitchen talking to someone on the phone.

"He did?"

"What was the time?" Steven could hear that his dad's voice was slightly trembling.

"Well, thank you for letting me know." Steven heard his dad hang up the receiver with a loud crash and yelling out, "Damn it!" and started crying. Elaine woke up and ran into the kitchen to see what was going on. Steven wanted to know too, so he walked in; he had never seen his dad cry before.

"Joe, what's wrong?" Elaine grabbed a chair so Joe could sit on it. Instead, he kicked it out of his way and got a bottle of whiskey and started to drink straight from the bottle.

"Joe, what's wrong?" Joe's eyes were red and watery and he leaned against the kitchen counter just taking swigs from the bottle while gently sobbing. Steven deep down knew what had happened but did not want to say it out loud. Steven grabbed his mom and left his dad in the kitchen.

"Steven, what happened?" Elaine sat on the couch looking at Steven who decided to stay standing.

"Well, I got up to go to the bathroom and as I was walking past the kitchen, I heard dad on the phone talking to someone. I saw that it was five in the morning and thought it was odd he would be talking to someone this early. I overheard him talking and after he finished, he hung up the phone and began crying. From what I gathered from the conversation, I think Uncle Chris passed away."

Steven looked at his mom. She lost her own brother several years back and even though she was not close to Chris, she had a deep understanding of losing a brother. Steven was hoping it would not set her off, but she sat there in thought.

"What a shame, I know how much your dad loved his brother, especially since their own father died when they were both young." Steven looked at his mom, he did not know his grandpa Thomas died when his father was young, he just knew his grandpa died before he was born.

"Dad never told me that, he has always told me stories about Uncle Christopher, I just assumed grandpa was never a part of it." Steven then sat next to his mother so they could talk quietly and Joe could not hear them.

"Your father was only fourteen when his father died. Your Uncle Christopher was eighteen, so when their father died, Christopher was like a father for your dad."

"That makes sense now. Dad always told me stories of what sounded like he was in his late teens and early twenties; it makes sense that grandpa was never in the picture." Steven looked down and felt bad for his father.

"Your father usually never talks about his own father, but he always does of Christopher and I understand why your dad is taking it so hard. Your uncle took care of your father until he turned legal age, but your father stayed with your uncle for several years so they could run a restaurant together."

"Yeah, dad told me about that."

"Oh, okay, I didn't know how much your father has told you." Elaine got up. "I'm going to go back to bed, I'm going to let your father have some space, I honestly don't think he wants anyone around him; it will probably make him angry." Then his mom walked back into the bedroom.

Steven sat there on the couch. That was the first serious conversation he has really ever had with his mother. He had talked with his mom before, but this time it was different, he felt like they talked to each other on a normal level. The last time, Steven really had a conversation with his mom was when he was younger. They mainly talked about kid-oriented things, but now that Steven was fourteen, he felt that he was able to have an adult conversation with one of his parents, let alone with his mom.

Steven took his mom's lead and went back into his own bedroom, since his father was drinking straight from the whiskey bottle. He did not want to piss off his dad when he was in this state. Besides, Steven understood wanting to be left alone, during a time like this. When he himself was depressed or sad about something, he usually wanted some time alone until he was ready to talk to someone about it. Instead of going back to bed, he turned on his TV and started to play some games.

A couple of hours went by and Steven heard his father snoring. He had heard his father snore before but usually it was not this loud. It sounded like a hog that could not breathe. It would start off loud then taper off into a faint sound, and then another loud hog suffocation and then release. Steven walked out of his room and noticed it came from the kitchen. He walked into the kitchen and saw his dad sitting on the kitchen floor with an empty bottle of whiskey and his head leaning into his chest. It made sense to Steven why his dad was snoring so loud; the way his head was positioned was restricting his airflow. Steven wanted to wake up his dad but decided not to; he just left him there to sleep off the whiskey.

Elaine came into the living room and saw Steven sitting on the couch.

"What are you doing in here; is your dad still in the kitchen sleeping?"

"Yeah, how did you know?"

"I did not go back to bed; I came out to check in on him every half hour to see how he was doing. He just fell asleep about half an hour ago." Elaine sat in the recliner and turned on the TV.

"What are you doing, you are going to wake him up."

"Well, I want him to get up but without waking him up myself." Elaine smiled at Steven. "Yeah, but you know how he has been lately, he'll probably get angry and yell at us for waking him up with the T.V."

"Oh, I know, but he can't just sleep in the kitchen all day." Steven sat there and thought that his dad could, and should, but he did not say anything more to his mom.

At noon, Joe finally woke up from his sad, drunken, morning binge. He staggered into the living room and saw Steven and Elaine watching TV together.

"I'm sorry you two had to see me like that." He walked slowly and slumped into the second recliner across the living room. "I'm guessing you might know what has happened?" Joe looked at Elaine and Steven and saw that they both just sat there silently. "Well, Christopher died after midnight. I knew it was going to happen soon, but not this soon. From what he was telling me, it sounded like he had another year or so. But I guess he didn't stop drinking and so his liver failed faster because of it."

"Wasn't he on the donor list?" Elaine said in a sympathetic tone.

"Yes, but since his cirrhosis was caused by alcohol, he was on the very bottom of the list. I was hoping that if he straightened himself out, quit, and showed he was really wanting to get better, he would get higher on the list, but instead he just kept drinking." Joe was staring at the floor with tears welled up in his eyes.

"I'm so sorry, Joe." Elaine got up to walk towards Joe.

"I know, but please, I just want to be left alone." Elaine understood and walked back towards Steven.

"Mom, is it okay if I go over to Mike's?" Elaine nodded and she went into the bedroom to watch TV. Joe sat in the chair and drifted back to sleep.

Three months had passed since Christopher passed away. It was summer vacation for Steven, and he spent most of his nights at Mike's house. Steven did this not because of his mother, but due to his dad. Ever since Christopher's passing, Joe had become increasingly angry, even more than before. Joe would yell and scream at Steven for the smallest of things. One day, Steven had left the refrigerator door open while looking for something to drink.

"Close that damn door; you should know what the hell you want before you open it. You are letting all the cold air out and wasting electricity." Steven heard his dad yelling from the living room.

"Sorry, Dad."

"No, you need to stop wasting electricity, you think money grows on damn trees?"

Steven stood there not saying anything. Joe got up and walked towards Steven.

"Answer me when I am talking to you!" Joe's yelling was so loud it rang in Steven's ears. His dad was so close to him, his father's alcohol spit spattered on his face.

"Sorry, Dad, I won't do it again."

"You're damn right, go to your room and make sure you turn off the damn light the next time you are not in it." Steven walked past his dad and could smell the stench of alcohol oozing out of his pores.

It was worse between his mother and father. His dad often times looked like he was going to hit his mom, but he had never seen or heard his dad do it. But the fights between them were bad. Elaine fought back, unlike Steven. Steven just took his dad's yelling and moved on, but Elaine would yell back at Joe and it would escalate the fighting even further. Steven was tired of all the yelling that was going on and decided to spend the nights at Mike's. Steven didn't know if his dad cared or not, but he didn't care; he did not want to be around his dad when he was like this. He did feel bad for his mother and leaving her there with his dad, but she seemed to keep herself busy with CARE and spending time with some friends from her CARE group. Joe worked most of the time anyway, so Elaine usually only had to deal with the yelling and fights in the evening, until Joe would pass out drunk on the couch.

Yet, Steven still felt bad about leaving his mom there with

his dad, but he did not want to be home with his parents at all. He was hoping that by the end of summer vacation, maybe some more time after his uncle's death, his father would hopefully recover enough to where he would not be constantly yelling or fighting with him and his mother.

"Steven, what do you want to do today?" Mike asked Steven while they were riding their bikes around the neighborhood.

"I don't know, whatever I guess."

"Oh, come on, man, I've had to pick for the last week, let's do something where I don't have to suggest for once." Mike was laughing, he was not angry at Steven, he knew what was going on at his house.

"How about I make a list and you can choose; that will ease it up from you, okay?"

Steven and Mike were passing by the mall. Steven saw a sign that read "Now Open, West Ridge Arcade." Steven thought that maybe playing some arcade games would help ease his mind.

"Hey, how about we go there?" Steven pointed at the sign and Mike smiled.

"That sounds like a good idea, I got twenty bucks on me, you?"

"I still got some cash from my grandma from my birthday earlier this year." Mike looked at him.

"Dude, your birthday was like six months ago, how much does your grandma give you?"

"She usually sends me two hundred."

"Still, I could blow that in a week buying video games or writing supplies."

"Well, it's because, if you haven't noticed, I buy my writing supplies from the dollar store. Also, I don't buy my games, because my dad gets me games for Christmas."

"Yeah, but doesn't he usually buy you only two? And for your birthday he buys you one, so you only get three a year."

"Don't forget I replay them over and over again, also the ones I don't like I usually sell. I'm surprised you haven't noticed that yet."

"That is true, I just never put two and two together."

"Yeah, I'm just really tight with my money, I usually carry over whatever my grandma gives me, plus she gives me money for Christmas too, I just don't tell anyone. That is how I usually always have money on me, I'm good at saving."

"Well, you okay with spending some at the arcade, Mr. Moneybags?" Mike gave a slight punch on Steven's shoulder.

"Yeah, yeah, say what you want." Steven just smiled and began to bike towards the arcade. Mike followed behind.

Steven and Mike got to the arcade and it was busy with kids, teens, and adults. They walked in and saw that it was very large and brimming with lights reflecting off retro, arcade machines from the eighties, some recent ones from the late nineties and recent arcade games like Dance Revolution. DDR was very popular and became a big fad with both kids and adults. Steven and Mike saw a large line behind two DDR games. They could hear the cheers and screams coming from the crowd that was gathering around both sets of players on the dance boards. They were both not very interested in playing, they were both wanting to play some retro classics like Pac-Man and Donkey Kong.

The smell of the arcade was satisfying to Steven. He could smell fresh pizza coming from the far end of the arcade where the restaurant was located. The smell of new carpet was faint, but Steven noticed it was a different kind of scent, like fresh from the flooring store type of smell. The atmosphere was abuzz with not only people but the sounds from the machines would fill the whole building. Steven would hear "Press Play Now" or "Game Over" repeatedly echo throughout the arcade. Steven felt he was whisked away in an electric joy land where he felt he could be lost for hours, without the world even noticing he was gone; he really liked that feeling.

Steven really enjoyed the fact that there was a sign that read "All Games before 2000 are only twenty-five cents ALWAYS!" Mike saw the sign and looked at Steven, both of them were excited, especially Steven, because he was very good at video games and knew that twenty-five cents would carry him for a long time. Mike was fairly good, but he knew Steven would probably get a lot farther with one quarter than he would. They both looked around and saw that besides the DDR game, a set of new car racing games, and some new recent shooting game that came out, most of the arcade was well-stocked with machines previous to 2000, which both Steven and Mike thought was funny because that was only three years ago.

Steven spotted a pinball section and saw two rows of six machines in each row. Steven never really played pinball but always heard stories of how his uncle and father would play pinball a lot back in their day. Joe would tell stories to Steven about back in the seventies when pinball arcades were very popular and were very similar to arcades today but that it was just all pinball machines, possibly a couple of pool tables or shuffleboards mixed in. Joe would tell Steven stories about how Uncle Chris would get the highest scores on some of the machines and that there were some pinball tournaments that his uncle won. Steven wanted to try pinball for himself.

"Hey Mike, you want to play some pinball? There is like twelve machines to choose from!"

Mike looked over and saw the two rows of machines; he also noticed that there were two of each which Mike liked, because he knew in pinball that if there are two players, they have to take a turn on the same machine. He figured the owner must of thought about this and is why there is a set of two for each pinball game.

"Sure, how about we both play the same type but on two different machines?"

"Yeah, that sounds awesome!"

Steven and Mike walked over to the pinball machines and chose one that looked interesting. It was a sci-fi themed machine that had a UFO spinning and abducting a man and woman. The top of it said, "UFO INVADERS." They both agreed to this one and each chose their machine.

Steven and Mike played for over an hour. Steven only went through two quarters while Mike went through four already. Mike would keep looking over at Steven's score and often times this distraction is what cost him a ball. Over time, Mike would slowly grow mad at the little, silver metal ball and would feel embarrassed by how badly Steven would be kicking his butt. Steven on the other hand did not look over at Mike's score, he was concentrating on the game. He felt he was matching the theme of the game and felt out of the world; he felt like he was carried away in some high that only this game could provide. He enjoyed the feel of the bumpers hitting the ball and feeling the vibrations from the ricochets caused by the mechanical bumpers that would bounce the ball back and forth, until the ball was spit back out towards Steven's two bumpers. Steven loved the lights when they flashed if he racked up huge points as well as the sound "EXTRA BALL" the machine would belt out when he would hit a certain score. Steven was both in the zone and felt free from his worries. Writing used to give him the feeling of being lost and disconnected from this world, but writing felt more like a chore than something he enjoyed. Lately, he was trying to write a piece that he wanted to be published in a magazine or win a contest that his school would submit in a student orientated contest, but he would get so hung up on his work that he never submitted because he would edit it to death until he just felt it was never good enough. So lately, it just did not help keep his mind off his personal issues, because, since his work did not feel good enough, he did not feel like he was good enough. But now, this pinball game was bringing him a feeling that he has not noticed in a long time—distraction from the world around him.

After another hour passed, Mike was getting bored of the pinball game.

"Hey, Steven, you want to go play something different?" Mike looked over and saw that Steven did not respond or even acknowledge him. Mike waited a couple of minutes and spoke louder. "Steven, you want to go to a different game?" Still no response, Mike was getting a little irritated. "Steven, yo, Steven, can you hear me?" He then began to approach Steven, until his cell phone rang in his pocket.

Steven was still entranced with his pinball game. He did not hear Mike calling out to him or the cell phone that Mike had in his pocket. Steven realized he was on the same quarter for over an hour. He finally looked up and saw that his score was not only the highest, but it was smashing the previous score by a mile. Steven began to smile and saw he still had one ball left and was hoping that he would be able to get an extra one by getting the next set that was required. He was about to hit the ball right into the center that led to a ramp where a score multiplier was held when Mike took his right hand off the button.

"Dude, what's up? I was about to get an extra ball." Steven looked over at Mike and was angry.

"Dude, your dad is on the phone, it sounds like an emergency." Steven looked at Mike and knew it had to be a pretty big deal. Joe did not have Mike's cell phone number.

"How did he get your number?"

"Your dad called my mom and told her it was an emergency, so she gave him my number. You should probably take it now." Steven grabbed the phone.

"What's up, Dad, what's wrong?"

"Steven, your mom has flipped out again." Steven's heart jumped into his throat. No matter how many times he had gone through this, he still could not take it.

"What happened?"

Steven stepped away from the pinball machine and heard

"Game Over." He looked and felt disappointed, even though he had a high score, he really wanted that extra ball.

"Steven, are you still there?" Steven could tell his dad was growing impatient over the phone.

"Yeah, sorry."

"Anyways, I tried calling your mom earlier today to see if she wanted me to bring anything to eat from work. I called and called, and she never answered. But she always calls back when she sees that the caller ID has my work's number. She never called back, so I thought that was strange. Well, I left it alone and came back home from work at five p.m. and saw that the car was still in the driveway. I thought maybe she was gone and just got home. I went inside and she was not there. I then went over to Cathy's house and she said she has not seen your mom all day. I don't know where she has gone; I found her address book and called all of her friends I could find and none of them said they have either heard or seen her today."

"Dad, Dad, slow down" Steven could tell his dad was talking really fast and sounded panicky over the phone.

"Did you call the cops?"

"Yeah, but they said they can't do anything until she is missing for over forty-eight hours."

"Well, maybe she went out for a walk or something."

"No, I thought of that and drove around the neighborhood for the past thirty minutes—I did not see her." Steven thought hard and could not think what else it could be.

"Steven, I need you to come home now so maybe we can find your mom together." Steven did not have to see his dad to tell that he was drunk; his father was talking really fast and his speech sounded off.

"Okay Dad, I'll be there in an hour."

"An hour? Where the hell are you?"

"I'm at the new arcade at the mall."

"Jeez, Steven, it's nearly eleven miles across town."

"I know, but Mike and I usually bike around town for a while and we got to this side of town and saw the arcade and wanted to check it out." Steven held out the cell phone to see what time it was. It read 7:10 p.m.

"I'll try to bike faster if I can, I promise."

"Well, hurry up, I need you here." Then Steven heard his dad hang up the phone.

"What's wrong?" Mike could tell on Steven's face that he went from worried in the beginning to frustrated.

"I don't know, my dad is freaking out because my mom is not home." Then Steven told him the conversation.

Steven and Mike were biking together.

"You sure you don't want me to come?" Steven looked over at Mike.

"Have I ever had you come before?" Steven said in a light voice, not in anger or aggression, but just in a tired voice.

"No," Mike looked down at his front tire.

"I'm sorry, Mike, I know you just want to help, it's just this is something I don't want to drag you into. It is nothing against you."

"I know, I know, don't worry about it, but just don't forget I would come if you ever invited me to."

"I know, and I appreciate your understanding."

Steven really did appreciate it, Mike never pushed Steven into going with him; Mike was just curious. He has always heard the stories but had never seen it in person. Mike did not think Steven ever lied about what happened with Steven's mother, but he always had a little nag to go see it in person. However, he respected Steven and would never do something that would make him feel uncomfortable or cause a loss of trust.

"Well, this is where we will separate, I'll call you if I think my dad and I need help." Mike knew it was not true but smiled at Steven and gave him a half hug that they did when they separated.

"Alright, I'll see you later."

"Okay," and Steven pedaled to his house.

By the time Steven got home, the sun had just set for the night. It was a clear, night sky, with no cloud coverage at all. The moon was full, but farther away. The bright, illuminous, white moon shone as bright as ever. The stars were twinkling and the backdrop of the single, large tree behind the house gave it a beautiful sense of tranquility and silence. Steven saw that the lights were on in all the rooms. Steven walked in the house and saw his dad passed out on the couch, with several empty beer cans on the coffee table. When he closed the door, he slammed it hoping it would wake up his dad. He saw his dad startle and jump up. "Elaine?" Joe then finally realized it was Steven standing in front of the door.

"Oh, about time you came." Steven looked at the clock hanging over the TV. "It's 7:55, I'm fifteen minutes early, I rode as fast as I could."

"Yeah, that is true. Sorry, I'm just worried about your mom, I don't know if she is flipping out somewhere and causing trouble or what." Steven began to wonder if his dad was more worried about his mom's well-being or just worried about how he might be viewed. Usually, his mom was able to get help without most of the neighbors knowing, but the first two episodes caused Joe embarrassment and he felt ashamed. Steven also knew that when his mom was sick, Joe was worried what she was telling the doctors about his drinking. Steven was wondering if his dad was more worried about what she might be saying to strangers. Also, when Elaine is sick her checks from social security could not be cashed, unless she signed them and cashed them in person. Joe did not put Elaine on his checking accounts in case during an episode she would try to drain all the money. Steven noticed that the past couple of years his mom would get out of the hospitals faster and drift in and out, but as long as she was there in person to cash the checks, Steven felt that was what his dad really cared about.

Steven looked at his dad and could not tell for sure if his dad was deeply concerned or not, but he could tell his dad was affected in some way.

"Well, I'm home now, what should we do next?" Steven could tell his dad was pretty drunk and that driving around some more was out of the question.

"Honestly, I don't know, I was hoping you would maybe have an idea." Steven was thinking when he saw out the kitchen window a shadow pass by. He ran to the window and looked out into the backyard; he did not see anything except for the shadow from the tree.

"What's wrong, Steven?" Steven heard his dad call out from the couch.

"I don't know, I thought I saw something." He was still looking at the backyard but could not see anything.

"You think it was your mom?" Joe was stumbling behind Steven.

"You, don't think she could be in the shed, do you?" Steven looked at the shed and a shudder ran down his back. The shed stood there and looked daunting. It was an old shed that used to be a house from the early 1900s that had a small garage attached. It was a single room that had the original pot belly stove that was once black but was now completely brown in rust. There were two shelves in the old kitchen area and now the ceiling was caving in. The roof was re-shingled before Joe bought the home and the outside was repainted and redone. However, the electricity was taken down and re-routed to the current home that was built in the 1950s, but instead of separating them into two separate homes, the old home, or the shed, was added onto the property as a rear garage, even though the garage door faced the back of the house and not the alley.

Steven did not want to go into the shed at night. He knew there was no electricity that ran to the shed anymore and that with its internal crumbling state, it was not ideal to go in at night. His family used it to put junk in it like old tires, decorations, and other oddities that filled up the house. But the darkness of the shed and it being nighttime is what got to Steven. Over the years, his fear of the night still had a hold on him. It was not as bad when he was with Mike and they would sometimes ride their bikes a little after sunset, but they usually were in the house when it was too dark. The moon's once bright light was now blocked by the large menacing tree that Steven thought was so tranquil not that long before. All Steven could see was the outline of the shed and the small single door that was always open.

"Do you really want me to go check in there?" Steven kept staring at the shed.

"Yes, go see if your mom is in there, maybe that shadow was her." Steven looked at his dad and was going to ask him to do it but saw that his dad's face was red and his eyes were glossed over. The smell of alcohol was pouring from his dad's breath. He knew his dad would not be able to go check, even with a flashlight. His dad would more likely fall down just going down the three steps from the back patio. Steven breathed in deep.

"I'll go check, let me get a flashlight."

Steven found a flashlight in the catch drawer in the kitchen. He flipped the switch and a dull yellow light came from it. The flashlight felt cold in his hands.

"Do we have a different flashlight, Dad?" Steven heard no reply and only heard snoring coming from the living room. His dad was already passed out on the couch again. When he walked towards the backdoor, he a saw an empty whiskey bottle in the trash.

"I knew he couldn't be drunk from just the beer cans I saw on the coffee table."

Steven shined the dull, yellow light into the back yard.

He left the kitchen door open just to make sure he didn't accidently lock himself out. He slowly approached the shed and kept the yellow beam straight on the shed door. The light was only strong enough to hit the front wall of the shed but barely filtered through the doorway as he approached. As he was walking closer, he heard a noise come from behind the tree. He froze and shifted the light towards the tree. The noise began to stir again, and Steven's heart began to pound. Suddenly, he heard a noise come from inside the shed and he shifted his light towards the doorway but the darkness inside swallowed the light. He heard the noise from behind the tree again and heard a stick lightly crack. Steven started to back up, then suddenly a loud shriek filled the air. Steven fell backwards and saw a cat skitter across the yard and run through the gap between the gate and fence.

"Come on Steven, get a hold of yourself." Steven stood up and heard a small noise come from the shed; Steven was really hoping maybe it was another cat inside the shed.

Steven slowly walked to the doorway of the shed and stopped at the opening. He shined his light into the single room. He moved the light from side to side. He saw some milk crates filled with his old toys off in the corner on the side of the entry way. He placed one foot into the room on the old concrete floor that had cracks sprawling in every direction. There was the pot belly stove and he noticed that the metal chimney that curved into the brick portion of the wall was hanging off to the side. It had been a couple of years since Steven had been in the shed, but he had always been in it during the day—at night it seemed ominous to him. He began to creep into the shed and looked around; the usual junk was still in here besides his old toys. There was a pile of old comforters laying to one side of the room that had a mound of dust on top. Off into the other corner were more milk cartons, with small oddities like old figurines, clothing, and some used pillows. He looked up and saw the old ceiling sagging with open spots where he could see old insulation. Then he looked and saw that there was the little nook where the kitchen used to be. He took in a deep breath and walked further into the shed, without the light it would be pitch black in here. The only window that the old house had was covered up by the paneling from the outside renovations that had been done to it before the property was bought by his dad.

Steven crept closer and his heart was pounding. He could tell that the flashlight was getting slippery in his hands from all the sweat. When he walked closer towards the nook, his right foot hit a large crack in the cement floor. He almost fell but caught himself on the old, pot belly stove. In doing so, he dropped the flashlight and it skidded away from him, with the light looking towards the doorway. After he regained his balance, he pushed away from the stove. Because of the force he put on the old stove, his weight knocked it over and it fell with a large crash and a large cloud of ash sprang into the air. Now, Steven's light was being choked out by the years-old gray ash and Steven began to cough uncontrollably. He bent down to pick up the flashlight and tried to look around but could not see anything, He wandered around trying to get back out of the shed but then he bumped into something soft; he then felt two hands on his shoulders. A chill ran down his spine and he pointed the flashlight to whatever was touching him. Then two, bright eyes reflected the dim light. He stood there frozen and all he could see was the set of unblinking eyes staring at him and then he heard a loud, "SHHH!" Steven backed away and saw that the ash was clearing up enough so that the moon's light, after moving just enough to glimpse through the doorway, allowed him to run towards it and he ran out as fast as he could. He did not look back, but he could feel a presence following him.

Steven ran into the kitchen and closed the door behind him. He could hear someone pounding at the door, but they were not saying anything. After a few minutes, the pounding stopped. Steven did not dare open the door but he went to the kitchen window to see who it was. He saw no one was at the door anymore and then he looked around some more in the backyard and saw nothing. Then suddenly, two hands began scratching at the window and he saw his mom bashing her forehead against the thick glass. Her face was covered in ash, and a repeated "thud, thud, thud," echoed into the kitchen. Steven did not know if his mom would be able to break through the window, but he began to walk backwards while staring at his mother pounding her head repeatedly against the window. Soon, her forehead began to bleed.

Steven ran into the living room screaming at his dad to get up.

"Dad, Dad! I found mom!" Joe woke up half groggily and looked Steven in the face. He could tell Steven was scared and breathing heavily. It took Joe a couple of seconds to come to his senses, until he heard something coming from the kitchen.

"What the hell is that?" They both heard it; it was Elaine scratching at the back door. Steven and Joe ran towards the kitchen window and saw the blood smeared on the glass. Joe and Steven looked over and saw Elaine clawing at the back door not saying a word. Elaine kept scratching the back wooden door, until her fingers began to bleed, leaving a mix of blood and tan marks from the paint that was scratched off. Elaine just kept clawing at the back door, still silent.

Danny Fields, from next door, was letting his dog out when he saw Elaine constantly clawing the back door. He always carried a flashlight in case his dog wandered too far off into the backyard. He turned his light on towards Elaine. It's heavy, piercing, white light shone brightly against Elaine's ash covered body. Danny walked towards the fence that stood between their yards and he could see the blood covering the window and the back door.

"Elaine, what's wrong?" There was no answer, she just stood there constantly clawing at the door without a sound.

"Elaine, it's me Danny." Danny knew about Elaine's mental history, especially since he witnessed the first one and knew this must be another one. He ran into the house and called 9-1-1.

Soon, the cops came and picked up Elaine. Joe was sober enough to tell them his side of the story. But it was Steven that had to tell them everything that had happened. While he was giving him his story, he could see his mother clawing at the window in the back of the police cruiser. Steven just stood there staring at her, until the two cops realized what was happening and ran to get her under control. The cops yelled back, "We'll get a statement later." They opened the door and cuffed her bloody hands behind her so she would stop scratching the window. The lights on the car turned off and the car drove off down the street. Off in the distance, the moon light was hitting the back of the car and Steven could see his mom hitting her head against the window.

EPISODE SEVEN

Another year had passed since Elaine's last episode. Steven had at this point grown numb to the episodes that seem to happen either yearly or bi-yearly. However, it did affect him when he slept. He had been waking up to more nightmares and some of them were very intense and life-like. There are times when he wakes up, he has to get out of bed, and check the house to make sure he is not still dreaming. Often times, he will just stay up the rest of the night and do things to keep his mind occupied.

Steven was on spring break and did not care if he did not get much sleep, because he could take some power naps during the day; usually his naps were short enough not to worry about nightmares or realistic dreams. He had started staying home more often and not spending so many nights at Mike's house, because he felt bad about keeping Mike up. Some nights, he would wake up Mike after having a nightmare. Mike was a light sleeper and many things woke him up. When Steven was having a nightmare, he would toss and turn and wake up sitting straight and breathing heavily. One night, Mike asked Steven to go see a doctor or someone who could help him with his night terrors, but Steven would always say:

"No, after what I see with my mom, never." Then he would shut the conversation down as fast as it started.

Steven knew his mother had a mental disorder but seeing his mother going in and out of hospitals, switching multiple medications and seeing what happened when she stopped taking them suddenly, he was always afraid to seek help. He was afraid he would turn into his mother. He knew deep down that his issues were far different than his mom's, but something kept gnawing at him and telling him to not seek help, because he knew that they would just give him medication. He just did not want to take meds at all. Steven was afraid that the medication would change his mood, his way of thinking and knew that many medications can make you feel like a zombie. During the day, he functioned fine; he just had to deal with the nightmares. Sure, he was tired for most of the day, but it was a tiredness he grew accustomed to and did not mind. He was still able to function and get decent grades in school, especially in English courses.

Steven and Mike had been working more on their writing and both decided that when they got out of high school, in which they were both sophomores, they were going to go to the same college together and major in English or Creative Writing. Mike wanted to be a high school English teacher and Steven knew he wanted to try to make a living from writing and possibly get his master's degree in creative writing, so he could teach at the college level. He was not entirely sure but knew he had a love for writing and wanted to utilize it more. Mike enjoyed writing but he was always more of the teaching type and Steven could tell Mike would be a great teacher. Mike would often times help Steven come up with new ideas for a story or how to use proper grammar and punctuation. Mike had a natural gift for helping and teaching and Steven always told Mike he would make a great educator.

Today, Steven was going to go over to Mikes and work on a new poem he had been writing and have Mike help him edit it. Steven wanted to send this piece off to a magazine that is paying a five-hundred-dollar grand prize for the winner and Steven wanted to win it. He was now fifteen years old and next year, after he turns sixteen, he wanted to get his driver's license and save up enough money to buy a car. During last year, he mowed neighbor's yards for money and had saved up about four hundred dollars. He knew he would have to get a small part time job to help save more for the car, but he figured that winning the contest would help him get closer to his goal.

As Steven was getting ready to head out to Mike's, the phone rang. He could hear his mom still sleeping in the bedroom, so he went to the kitchen and answered the phone. It was his Aunt Margret, his dad's sister. Joe had talked very little about his sister, Margret, other than saying that she was a very mean lady and that she did not want to do anything with Joe or his family. Steven wondered why his dad hated his own sister so much, but Steven had only talked to his aunt once in his life and that was when he was very young. He did not remember much about her except for her high-pitched, whining, New York accent and she always talked fast and to the point. Steven could hear that high-pitched tone over the phone and realized that it was definitely her.

"Hello?" Steven asked politely.

"Is Joe there?"

"No, he is at work. This is Steven, his son."

"Hi, Steven." Steven could tell that she seemed in a hurry. "Well, when you see your dad, tell him that his mom is dead." Steven's heart jumped into his throat and he felt his balance give way. He had to lean against the wall to keep himself from falling.

"Grandma died?" Steven began to swell up with tears.

"Yeah, she died yesterday from a stroke. Let your dad know the funeral is tomorrow." "Wait, what?"

"I have to go, let your dad know and he can call me. Bye." Then she hung up.

Steven sat there, with the receiver in his right hand, tears swelling in his eyes, but also anger. Now Steven knew why his dad hated Aunt Margret so much. Who calls and talks like that? She did not sound like she was sad at all, there was no remorse in her voice, nothing. She talked as if it was something casual and she did not care. And then the funeral is tomorrow? Steven was wanting to know how they got the funeral set up so fast. Did she really die yesterday, or did she die previously and Margret is just now telling them? Steven knew his grandma had health issues lately and that her health was declining for the past year, but he did not expect this so suddenly and did not like how he had to receive it. "His mom is dead" kept sounding in his ears. He could not believe that his dad's own sister would say "his mom" like that—so casual and yet callused. Steven cried in both sadness in anger. How could someone speak so coldly about their own mother dying like that? Either way, he did not care about his aunt at all now and knew that he would never want to see or talk to her again.

Steven snapped out of his spell and decided to call Mike and let him know what had happened and that he was not going to come over today. He would come over tomorrow or the next day. After an hour, Elaine got up and Steven told her what had happened. "Oh no, Jasmine passed away?" Steven could tell his mom was affected by it too. She knew how much Joe loved his mom, but she knew how much Steven loved her too. Elaine knew that she had been gone because of sickness throughout the years but did not remember her schizophrenia. She always remembered her stays at the hospitals due to depression or being bi-polar, never having illusions or anything similar. But Jasmine took care of Steven when she was away when he was young and was like a mother to Steven. Elaine was always grateful for that.

"Are you okay, Mom?" Steven could tell his mom was about to break down and cry. When she cried, she cried like the world was about to end, part of it was due to her medication side effects and Steven knew it, but he always hated seeing her cry, because it was so emotional and heart wrenching. Also, he wanted to bawl, too, and did not want to do it in front of his mother.

"Yeah, yeah, I will be okay," Elaine wiped her tears with her sleeve, her blonde hair sticking to her cheeks.

"You sure, Mom?"

"Yeah, I'll be fine, I should call your dad and let him know."

"No, wait till he gets home, and matter of fact, I'll tell him for you."

"You sure, Steven?"

"Yes, Mom, I'll tell him. Besides, it was I who answered the phone, I can tell him in greater detail on how Aunt Margret handled it, so he'll direct his frustration to her."

"Yeah, that is a good idea." Steven looked at his mom and could tell that maybe she was not going to cry as badly as he thought. He looked at her and decided to give her a hug, partly because he wanted one.

Elaine saw Steven approaching and she did not know why.

"Are you okay, Steven?" Steven just approached her with his arms out and gave her a hug. They had not hugged much, not because Elaine never wanted too, she always wanted to hug her son, but he always seemed to never want any affection from her. She knew she was not in his life much, but when she was, she tried really hard to be a mother for him. Steven knew it too. He knew that when she was normal and not having episodes or times leading up to one, she was a good mom. He just hated getting attached to something he knew would just be thrown away and recycled all over again. But this time it was different. Steven needed to comfort his mom and he needed comfort, too. Steven was very close to his grandmother and loved her dearly. He would often call her at least once a week just to talk to her and see how she was doing. The last time he talked to her, she seemed okay and in good spirits and he felt his grandma was going to live long enough to see him graduate in two years, but now it would not happen and he felt torn by it.

Soon, they were in an embrace that Steven never had before. His mom held him tight and he could feel her warm breath hitting the top of his brown hair. She was holding him tight and swaying side to side saying, "It will be okay, Steven, it will be okay." Steven just nodded his head in her lower shoulder and cried. He cried for what seemed like half an hour, but it was only for a few minutes. They stood there in silence, until Steven finally gave way and backed up. They looked at each other and smiled. Elaine went into the kitchen and Steven could hear pots and pans rattling onto the stove.

"You want some breakfast? I know it is a little late in the morning, but I can make some bacon, eggs, and toast if you want?" Steven stood there and could feel his stomach rumbling.

"Yeah, that sounds great. I'll eat in the kitchen with you." Elaine stood their smiling knowing that her son needed her, and she loved that she could help.

It was six o'clock when Joe came home, and Steven and Elaine were in the kitchen together making dinner. Joe could smell the fresh pasta sauce that Elaine was making from scratch. He could smell the extra basil, because that was his favorite in the sauce. Joe walked into the kitchen and saw Steven helping his mom finish up. Joe could tell that something was up but could not tell what. He saw that Steven and Elaine were silent but he did not know why. Soon Steven put the plates on the table and plopped on large amounts of pasta on the three plates. Elaine then walked over with the pan of sauce and generously spooned large amounts of sauce on each mound of pasta. Joe looked at them both. "This all smells so good, what's the big occasion?" He had never seen Steven cook with his mom and part of him liked to see his son spend time with his mom, but he also knew something must be wrong. Steven looked at Elaine and she nodded back at him.

"Dad, I got some news to tell you," Joe looked at his son with stern eyes.

"Oh no, this is not a great way to start my night. What happened? You get in trouble in school?"

"No, I'm on spring break." Joe had been working a lot with his new job at Wendy's, as the general manager and even though he was off by six o'clock, he still worked ten-hour shifts, six days a week, with only Sundays off.

"Sorry, I forgot, well, what the hell is wrong, I had a long day." Joe has always had long days and what it really meant was he did not drink all day at this new job so he wouldn't get fired and now all he wanted to do was get some food in his stomach so he could down some beers and watch TV, till he passed out.

"Well, I don't know how to put this, but Aunt Margret called this morning." As soon as the name came out of Steven's mouth, Joe's face turned red in anger and disgust.

"What the hell did she want? She knows how much I hate talking to her." Steven could sense the resentment in his dad's voice against his own sister.

"She um . . ." Steven looked down towards the floor and tears began to well up in his eyes. They were still puffy from this morning and he could tell the tension was refilling under his eyes.

"Steven, what's wrong, what happened?"

"Grandma passed away." Steven closed his eyes and waited

for his dad to yell at him like it was his fault. But Joe just stood in silence. Steven looked up and could see his dad was just standing there like a statue. He said nothing and did not move. Steven did not like the tension that was building up in the room. Then Joe looked over at Steven and came and hugged him. Steven did not expect this at all, not only did he hug his mom, but now his dad was hugging him. Joe did not say anything; he just stood there and hugged his son. Joe knew how much Jasmine meant to not just himself but for Steven as well. Joe knew he was not the best dad in the world and new that Elaine was not around much. Joe also felt Jasmine was the good role model that Steven had growing up and he knew Steven was just as torn as he was. Steven wrapped his arms around his dad and cried softly, he could hear his dad quietly sobbing, but did not make another sound.

After a few minutes Joe backed up.

"How did it happen?" Joe sat down on the kitchen chair.

"She had a stroke yesterday." Joe looked down and rubbed his hands through his thin black hair. Steven could see that his dad was beginning to sweat, and it collected on his dad's light wrinkles, due to years of heavy drinking and working long hours over the years.

"I see, . . ." is all Joe said. Then Steven felt he had to tell his dad how Margret told him, so he told his dad how the conversation went. After Steven was done, Joe got up, with anger in his eyes.

"You're telling me she died yesterday but the funeral is tomorrow? She knows sure in hell I could not make it to New York in time for the funeral, let alone afford to fly up there.

She has the nerve!" Joe ran towards the phone and began dialing it.

"Margret! This is Joseph, what the hell happened to Mom?" Steven and Elaine just stood there and heard Joe yell back and forth with his sister. After a couple of more minutes of yelling, Joe finally hung up the phone.

"That asshole, she lied to me. Grandma did not die yesterday, she died three days ago. She did not feel like it was the right time to tell me because she felt guilty having to tell me." Joe began to pace back and forth, yelling out swear words.

"She did not feel guilty, this is her way at being an asshole to her own brother. The nerve she has to do this to me. I hope she feels great about it." Steven looked at his father, his suspicions were correct, he knew a funeral was too quick, especially after saying it was a stroke.

"Joe calm down, you need to settle down." Elaine picked up the plate of pasta.

"Come on, it's your mom's recipe, I thought you would enjoy it."

As soon as Joe heard this, he stopped pacing and looked at the steaming plate.

"Mom's recipe?" Joe muttered; he began to calm down and sat down at the kitchen table. Steven and Elaine sat down at the table and began to eat; they all ate in silence, but knew Joe deep down appreciated this, because they never ate at the table together, but Joe did with his brother and mom when Margret moved out of the house, after Joe's father passed away.

Two months had passed since Jasmine's death and Joe had taken it very hard. Just like when his brother, Christopher, died, after Jasmine's death, Joe had been drinking heavily and taking out his frustration on both Elaine and Steven. It was now summer vacation for Steven and he had still been more at home than he had been sleeping over at Mike's house. Steven still went over to hang out during the day but went home so he could help support his mother emotionally. The last time Steven slept over at Mike's house after Uncle Christopher died, he felt guilty leaving his mom with his father knowing that his dad was taking out his frustration on his mom, since no one else was home to take the brunt of the verbal abuse.

Steven would bear the brunt of it when his dad got home, but it was just all verbal and was about things that were very minor, so Steven could just shrug it off. Since it was summer vacation, Steven did not have to worry about school being a topic. Even though Steven was doing well in school, his dad would pick something minor such as coming home late, not checking in before going to Mike's house, or possibly having a grade slip. But at least with vacation in place, it was one less thing his dad could yell about. Often times, Joe would get home and Elaine would have dinner ready, so it would be one less thing for him to get mad about. Usually, Joe was upset over small things such as a certain shirt was not washed or if not all of the dishes were clean. When he yelled at Steven, it was over things like not having his room all the way cleaned or not helping more with the chores, even though Joe knew that if Steven was not over at Mike's, he was out mowing lawns for some extra cash. But Joe would get mad if Steven forgot to take off his shoes, before coming into the house and tracking green mark stains from the grass cuttings. Steven did not mind, he knew his dad would never hit him and that he was all bark; he was just glad he was able to deflect it from his mom towards himself.

Joe's drinking increased and he began to drink at work again. He hid it from the employees by going into the walk-in cooler where he hid his drink behind boxes, at the back of the walk-in. He would go in whenever the kitchen needed things like produce or shake mix for the machine. This was a way for him to go in and take a drink but still come out with something, so it looked less suspicious. The employees never questioned it because none liked to go in the cooler and bring back the food, since the cooler was at the very back of the kitchen, plus, when they were busy with lunch rush, Joe was able to replenish the front line without having to disrupt any of the other employees. Joe was very good at his job and always made monthly bonus and quotas, so the district manager never said anything. Joe suspected that the district manager may have suspected something about Joe's drinking problems but Joe was too good at his job and always made numbers so the district let it slide. He figured, until Joe did something wrong that was out in the open, he would just let it go.

Joe felt comfortable with his job and knew that he was able to get away with what he was doing. He had over twenty jobs in the past ten years and each time was fired for his drinking. This time he found a job where his work was so appreciated that the upper's did not care, as long as he still made his numbers. But Joe was careful to not drink too much on the job; he made sure to not get drunk, just enough to get him through until he got home. He could then drink however much he wanted.

Joe knew he was depressed that his mother passed away and had been most of his life. He felt he was too man enough to go seek help and always turned to drink to help with his demons of the past. He had never told Steven about his past and how he was in the gang life back in New York, with his brother, Chris. He does not want Steven to know about his past life; he knows that Steven is bothered by his drinking and does not want another thing for his son to be disappointed about. At least, he can blame drinking for not being in much of Steven's life and not telling him the truth—the fact that he had to move from New York and start a new life because of bad choices that he and his brother made.

No, Joe would not tell Steven about his past and he will not go see a doctor. He felt that drinking was the only option to stay sane and not to drag Steven down even further by knowing the truth about his father. Joe deeply loved Steven and made sure he was provided for with food and clothing and did wish he could spend more time with his son but Joe did not have a degree or a trade skill and working in restaurants as a manager is all he knew. Joe felt he was too old now and could not afford to go back to school even if he wanted to. So, he knew that he would not ever be able to be more in his son's life than he already was. By the time he arrived home from work, he was too tired to do anything other than watch TV and that was really the only time he spent with Steven by watching sports. Now, Steven does not really enjoy watching baseball or football anymore and Joe does not like other shows besides the news, so they don't really talk much unless he is yelling at Steven. Joe felt guilty about this but he had no one to talk to and does not have friends to rely on. His brother is dead as well as his mother who would always listen to him vent. Now the only way he could get his frustration out was by yelling at Steven or Elaine.

Joe did deep down love Elaine, but, at the same time, he was afraid to get close to her. He felt that he damaged their relationship too much to really get close together. He knew that Elaine loved him, but he was afraid to show his love back due to all the fights that they have had and the fact that he knows he would not change no matter how much he tried. He knew if he quit drinking that maybe they would be closer but, without alcohol, he did not know how he would really function, so it has always been a vicious cycle of drinking and relying on it to stay where he was. He was content knowing that Elaine wouldn't leave, mainly because she wants to be with Steven and be more in his life. Joe was starting to get a chill; he noticed that he was in the walk-in cooler far too long and his hands began to tingle and his ears were getting red. He hoped that no one would really notice that he was gone far too long, so he walked out with the bags of chicken breast he came for. It seemed that no one cared that he was gone for twenty minutes.

It was towards the end of summer vacation and Steven had not heard from the contest he entered back in April. The contest said it would finish reading entries the first of July and it was now the first of August. He and Mike had not heard anything yet. Mike entered too because he wanted a shot at the prize money but said he would be happy with second place which was two hundred fifty dollars. Steven was watching TV when the phone rang. He wondered who would be calling. His mom was out at a doctor's appointment and he was alone, so he ran to the kitchen and answered the phone.

"Hello?" he was panting from running across the house towards the phone; he really wished he had a cell phone like Mike did.

"Is this Steven Thomas?" a young girl asked over the phone. Steven could tell that she was really young, probably not much older than him.

"Yes, this is he."

"Hi, my name is Stacey, with Kansas Quarter Magazine." Steven's eyes opened wide; this was really a coincidence, since he was just thinking about it. His heart began to pound, and his hands became sweaty. He knew that they would be calling to let him know the results and he was afraid he did not make the top three. He was willing to settle for the third place of one hundred dollars—just getting published in this magazine would be a great feat.

"I am calling to let you know about the results of the contest you entered." Steven stood there silently, nodding his head over the phone as if she could see him.

"Well, we are letting you know that your piece, 'The Ballad of a Teenager,' has placed first in our contest and that you will be receiving the winning five hundred dollars and published on our first page as our 'New and Upcoming Poet' featurette. I am verifying that you agree to this?" Steven held the receiver between his hands and started to jump up and down in excitement screaming "yes! yes! yes!" What he didn't realize is that Stacey could still hear him. "Oh, I'm sorry," feeling embarrassed, he settled down and collected himself.

"Yes, I accept!" he could not contain his excitement.

"Okay, I just wanted to verify some information so we can send your check in the mail and a copy of the magazine for you." She asked him the questions and he verified and told her the information he sent with the entry was still up to date.

"Well, thank you and congratulations." Steven hung up the phone and immediately called Mike to let him know.

"Wow, congrats, Bro!" Steven could tell that Mike was happy for him but sounded sad over the phone.

"What's wrong Mike?"

"Well, right before you called, they called me ten minutes ago and told me that I got fourth place." Steven could tell that Mike sounded deflated.

"That's still a pretty good achievement, there were like over one hundred entries, plus fourth and fifth place still get published in the magazine."

"Yeah, but it doesn't sound as good as 'Hey, I won a writing contest' or even at least 'I was runner up' or heck even third. It wasn't for the money honestly, I just wanted to have it on my list of achievements, so I had a chance at a scholarship for college."

Steven could tell that Mike was down and he did not want to keep praising him; he knew that if Mike just thought it over, he would realize getting published in the magazine was an achievement in itself. Steven heard the front door open and saw his mom coming in.

"Hey, I got to go, my mom just got home from the doctor, I'll call you later, okay?" "Yeah, I'll talk to you later, see ya." Steven felt bad for Mike, but he knew he would soon come to his senses. Steven was still floating from his win and wanted to tell his mom.

Steven saw his mom come in the door and sit down on the couch. He could tell something was up with her; she was sitting there staring off at the TV. He walked in the room and saw that the TV was still off and that the remote was still on the coffee table.

"Mom, are you okay?" he looked at her and saw that her blond hair was clean and straightened. His mom always dressed nicely and extra clean for doctor's appointments. He never knew why; he just figured it was just another thing to do in the day and never understood why someone would get dressed extra nice as if they were going to church but instead to a doctor's appointment.

Elaine still sat there in silence staring at the TV.

"Mom, everything go okay at the doctor's appointment?" Still silence. Steven got in front of the TV hoping that breaking the stare would help. When he got in front of his mom, he saw that her head slowly shifted towards his direction. *Good*, he thought.

"Mom, what's wrong." He saw his mom's lips move but did

not hear anything. "What did you say?" he moved in closer to hear what she was saying. As he moved in closer, he could faintly hear what she was saying.

"Mom, can you please speak up, I cannot hear you, please tell me what is wrong." Steven began to worry, he was hoping his mom did not have some life altering news; he could not deal with another death so soon or if ever.

He approached closer and finally heard what she said. "I have diabetes." Steven stopped and stood there. He has seen some kids at school who has diabetes and heard of parents who had it. He knew it was something that was not curable but was manageable.

"Oh, it's okay, Mom, I'm sure they will give you some insulin or medications to help manage it." He then sat next to his mom to try and comfort her. He gave her a hug sitting by her side, but she just sat there unmoved.

"I have diabetes," she said again.

"I know, Mom, but like I said, it's manageable." He gave her another hug, but again nothing in return.

"I have diabetes," she repeated again. Steven knew what was going on, he had seen this before; he knew that this was the start and he had to think of a way to get her help. Steven got up from the couch and headed to the kitchen, so he could get his dad home and get his mom help, before it was too late. Then suddenly, Steven heard his mom yell across the room. "Stop! I have the cure, they just don't know it yet. I will cure myself!" Steven walked back into the living room and saw his mom still sitting there. Now she was looking at Steven, with a cold and angry stare.

"You heard my secret didn't you!"

"What?" is all Steven could muster.

"YOU HEARD IT! YOU HEARD I CAN CURE DISEASES!" Before he could realize it, his mom jumped up out of the couch and ran towards him. He sidestepped and his mom ran past him.

"Mom, you are not feeling well, we need to get you help."

"No, I can cure myself!" Steven knew she thought he was talking about her diabetes and not her mental state.

"Mom, listen, it's me, Steven." Elaine lunged at Steven with her whole body and Steven side stepped again; this time Elaine landed on her stomach and rolled over on her back. Staring at Steven with ice-cold eyes, they penetrated Steven to the core. He knew his mom was not there; she was someone completely different, no matter how much he told her who he was, he knew she would not recognize him. He was someone completely different to her. Elaine got up and Steven began to run towards the back door. Then something hard hit him in his back and before he knew it, he was pressed up against the back door, with something heavy behind him. He turned his head around and saw his mom pressing the kitchen table against his back. The edge was pressing right above his tail bone and the pain was intense. He felt that the wind was knocked out of him and he could barely breathe, his whole body was pinned against the wall and he could barely move. Steven didn't know what to do. He knew he had to get out of the house and get help for himself and for his mom. He thought how his dad would play along with Elaine and it usually seemed to work.

"Te . . . tell me about this cure," he said between clenched teeth.

"Never, only I know it and I will only use it on myself, no one needs to know!" Steven knew she would most likely not tell him, but he realized that this ample time decreased her strength, just enough for him to slip to underneath the table. Elaine realized what had happened and dropped to the ground. Steven saw his mom get on her stomach and she began to crawl towards him. He then pressed his back against the bottom of the table and jumped up flipping the table off of him and over his mom.

Taking advantage of his mom's dazed state, he turned around and ran out the back door. Steven ran towards the gate at the side of the house and ran along the south side of the house. His plan was to run across to Cathy's house and have her call the police, at this stage of her episode. The neighbors fence ran parallel to Steven's house up towards the front of the house. There was a narrow strip of yard between Danny's fence and their own house. He began to bolt across it when his mom jumped into the opening.

"You will not tell anyone about my secret, no one!" Steven saw his mom charging towards him and so he jumped across the fence into Danny's yard. He then ran out the back gate that led to the alley way. He could hear his mom still screaming in the background. He turned around and saw that she was still by their house. He stopped running to catch his breath; he saw that his mom turned around and ran back inside the house.

Soon Steven got to Cathy's house and told her what happened. He told her everything and she called the police.

Soon, they came and knocked on the door of their house. Elaine would not open the door. Since she was not a danger to herself at the moment, the officers said to call them back when Joe was home, since he had a key to get in. Steven did what the officers suggested and waited on the front porch of Cathy's, making sure his mom did not leave the house until Joe got home. Steven told his dad what happened.

When Joe got home, he opened the front door and to his surprise, Elaine was just sitting on the couch saying,

"I have diabetes."

All Joe said was "I know, let's get you back to the doctor to see what they can do." To Steven's surprise, she went out of the house and climbed in the truck with Joe. Steven saw the truck drive down the road and heard Cathy talking on the phone. "Yeah, she left willingly, you don't have to come back, thank you."

EPISODE EIGHT

Another year had passed since the last episode with Elaine. Steven's nightmares are still the same and the last episode is just another one added to his rolodex of nightmares that his mind likes to choose and process. Joe's drinking was still as heavy as before but Steven had noticed that his dad's health has been catching up with him. His father has been gaining weight and looked swollen in some places on his limbs. Joe, however, did not seem to be too affected by it. His dad still worked ten-hour days as the general manager at the fast-food restaurant. Steven had to say he was impressed with his dad. This had been the longest tenure he has had in a job for as long as Steven could remember.

One morning, Steven woke up early in the morning to use the restroom and he saw his dad passed out on the couch in the living room. He stood there looking at his dad snoring away. Steven could tell that his dad's snoring was heavier than usual and he figured it must be from the weight. Joe's legs were slightly poking out from underneath the blanket covering him from his neck down and Steven saw that his dad's legs looked swollen and were a slight pinkish color compared to the rest of his skin. Steven grew worried that something was wrong with his dad but did not want to bring it up and make his dad mad. He shrugged it off, went to the restroom, and went back to bed.

Steven woke up a couple of hours later with the sun shining on his face and a cool breeze blowing in through his half-opened window. He inhaled the smell of blooming flowers and heard the birds chirping outside, singing their happy song of romance. Steven got out of bed and checked the calendar and saw that it said "March 22nd," the first day of spring. He always enjoyed the first day of spring, not only because it was spring break but because it meant that winter was dead and spring is alive. Steven seemed happier during the spring and summer time and liked that the sun was out more and enjoyed the warmer weather. He always hated the cold and did not like riding his bike or walking in cold weather; he always dreaded going outside when there was snow and especially when the biting wind would cut through his jacket, no matter how many layers he had on.

But this spring break was different; he was now sixteen and it meant he could go get a job and his driver's license. The past year he was learning to drive with his mom. She would let him use her old, white, Ford Escort. They would go to the local park's parking lot and Elaine would let him drive around the lot and learn how to park, turn, and brake. The lot was very large and most of the time it was empty, so it was a great place for Steven to learn without worrying about getting into accidents on the road or injuring anyone. Steven felt confident that he would pass his driver's test. His goal for this week was to get his driver's license and then get a job.

Steven went to his mom's bedroom and saw that she was getting up out of bed.

"Hey, Mom, can we go to the DMV and get my driver's license?" Elaine rubbed her eyes and looked over at Steven.

"Sure, let me get ready, I'll even let you drive there if you want?" Steven looked at his mom and smiled,

"Yeah, that would be great, it will give me a little practice before I take the driving test." Elaine smiled back at him and then walked to the oak dresser and got some clothes.

"Is it okay if I take a shower first, Steven?"

"Yeah, I'll get my clothes on and look over the practice test one more time."

After Elaine finished getting ready, Steven just finished looking over his practice test and felt confident he would pass. He had taken the practice test over and over so many times that the answers were ingrained into his mind. He was told by Mike that the practice test questions were identical to the real test and that just memorizing the answers was enough. Steven was a little jealous that Mike got his driver's license first and that Mike's mom had a second car that she was able to let Mike drive. Mike hated the car because it was an old, early '80s Buick and Mike thought that it was ugly as hell. But he figured it was a set of wheels he could use to get around and Steven and Mike rode around in it often to school and back and went to the mall to hang out. Mike would usually park at the end of the parking lot so no one would see what he was driving but everyone knew that he drove the old, beat up, ugly Buick. He just wanted to deny it to keep himself happy.

Steven and Elaine got to the DMV around noon. Steven walked in and saw that it was very plain and seemed a little run down. There was a large line at the front desk with many teenagers his age; they must have had the same idea and waited until spring break to get their license.

"Steven, I'll go find a seat for us to sit, stand in line to get your ticket."

"This is the line just for the ticket?" Elaine chuckled,

"Yes, you get a number and then when they call it you will then take your written test and if you pass you go on to the driver's test."

Steven looked at the line and looked over towards where everyone was sitting. He sighed and figured it will take a while before he gets to his test.

"Well, after I get our number why don't we go get some lunch to pass the time, I think this will take a long time."

"Good idea, I'll wait here until you get your number."

Steven stood in line for twenty minutes, until he finally heard the "next" monotone voice that rung over the line speaker next to the ticket machine. Steven grabbed his number—"107." He looked at the screen that read "Now serving number 81" and he knew it would probably be another hour or two before his number would be called.

"Okay, Mom, we have twenty-six people ahead of me; let's go get some lunch, I think we should have enough time." Steven smiled and looked at his mom.

"Okay." Elaine got up and then they went to go grab a bite to eat.

After an hour and a half they returned to the DMV and

as soon as they walked in Steven heard "Now serving number 106." Steven was surprised that he was only one away; he thought that they would be just now getting to the late 90's by now.

"Well, I guess your number will be next. I'm going to sit down." Elaine found a spot and grabbed a magazine to read.

Steven just stood up because he knew that he would be next soon, since it seemed to go quicker than he thought. Before he knew it, "Number 107" sounded over the speaker system. Steven walked up and was greeted by an older lady that wore thick, framed glasses and seemed uninterested.

"Are you number 107?"

"Yeah," Steven handed her the ticket.

"Okay, here you go, you have one hour to finish the test. When you are done bring it back and we'll look at it."

"Okay, thank you." Steven grabbed the test. He did not need an hour; it would take him fifteen minutes tops to finish this test. He has done the practice test so many times, he knew he would not need a whole hour.

As Steven figured, after he checked off the last question, he saw it only took him about seventeen minutes to finish the test. He walked back over to the same lady he had spoken to and handed her the test. She did not look up; she just took the paper and shifted her glasses down to her nose. She looked down at it and looked over the answers.

"You passed, here is your ticket for the driving test." Steven took the ticket and sat by his mom.

"How did it go?"

"Good, I passed, now I have to wait to take the driving test."

"What number are you?"

"Oh, just the same number—107." Steven sat there and waited. He was a little nervous; the written part was the easiest part but the driving test he was worried about. He did not know how strict they were with grading and worried that he would fail the driving portion. He had driven many times with his mom but most of the time in the park parking lot; he did not have much experience on the open road. Today was the farthest he had driven from his house on the streets.

"107" echoed across the lobby—it was a male voice. "Ugh, I guess this time a human announces the driving portion," Steven chuckled to himself. He walked up to the counter and saw an old man with gray hear, shorter than Steven and wearing a plaid, red shirt. He looked at Steven. "Are you 107?" The old man kept his eyes on his clipboard writing something down.

"Yeah, here is my ticket." Steven handed the man his ticket. The man still kept his eyes on the clipboard.

"Okay, follow me," he said in a monotone, casual voice. Steven could tell this was probably the man's millionth time doing this and this was just all mechanical to the man.

They stepped outside into the mid-afternoon sun.

"Okay, where is your car?"

"Over there, the white, Ford Escort."

"Okay, let's go." They walked towards the car and got in. Steven made sure to put his seatbelt on first and then started the car. He placed his hands at the appropriate locations and could tell in the corner of his eye that the old man was writing down every move that Steven was making. Steven made sure to keep his eyes on the road and not look over at the man.

Steven finished up the driving test in less than ten minutes, all he had to do was go down the street one mile, get on the highway, merge, get off, make a left turn, a right turn, and park back in the parking lot. It took ten minutes and Steven was surprised it did not take longer than this. He thought they would be driving around the whole town or at least do it for half an hour and not ten minutes.

"Okay, you passed." The old man handed him a piece a paper.

"Take this to the counter and they will take your picture. You will receive your official license in two weeks. In the meantime, you will have a temporary paper copy." The man handed Steven the piece of paper and walked out of the car. Steven was happy he passed and got the first thing checked off his list. Now it was time to go find a job.

It did not take long for Steven to find a job at a locally owned, fast food, hamburger joint called Top City Burgers. It was a staple in Topeka for over sixty years and they were always busy. Steven was surprised he was offered the job then and there. He thought it would take a while to call him back and let him know but the interviewer said that they were short staffed and thought that Steven seemed to be a good kid, so they told him he would be working 5 p.m. to 8 p.m., Wednesday through Saturday. Steven thought that twelve hours would be enough to help save up for a car. He figured he would use his mom's car until he had enough money to get a car and he knew, after he got his car, he would have enough hours to cover his insurance and gas and a little left over to do whatever he wanted. It would not be much extra, but he just really wanted his own car, so he could go wherever he wanted, whenever he wanted.

Steven juggled his new job and school pretty well. He did not spend as much time with Mike as he would like. They usually hung out when Steven was off, and Steven asked Mike if he would like to work with him.

"Nah, it's okay, I really don't need a job, my mom has a discounted car insurance rate where it is combined with my hunk of junk. The only thing I really have to pay for is gas which I just work for by doing chores around the house for my mom. Besides, I have been busy trying to get my grades back up, so I can get a scholarship for college."

Steven knew he should be doing the same thing; they would be graduating in less than two years. Steven's grades did not suffer while working his new job, but he did not have much time to write which he knew was his real chance at getting a scholarship. Mike was always a straight A student, and Steven was more a low B student and knew that his real chance at a scholarship was through his writing not his grades.

Another year passed and Steven was now seventeen. Steven was getting pretty comfortable with his life and realized it's been over two years, since his mom had an episode—the longest without one. The only thing that bothered him though was his dad; his dad's mood seemed to be more mellow, but his dad's health was really falling quickly. His dad was slowing down and was even drinking less. Steven was happy his dad was not drinking as much but knew it was due to something happening to his dad. His dad still worked his shifts but would come home so tired and beat from work, he would eat, drink one beer and then sleep all night without waking up, which was very unusual for his father. Besides his father's questionable health, Steven enjoyed everything else that had been going on with his life.

His mother the past two years had been pleasant; he felt like he had a true mom for once. She helped him with his driver's license, let him use her car to get back and forth to work and helped him shop around for a car that he finally had enough money to buy. It was a 1996 forest green Saturn and Steven got it for a good deal. His mom helped haggle the dealer down almost a grand and this left him some money left over so he could buy some writing supplies. The previous summer vacation he focused on writing so he could get scholarships for college and at the start of senior year, he won a writing contest that granted him enough money to cover the first two years of school. He felt happy and that life was finally going his way.

On a Saturday morning, after staying up all night finishing a short story that he hoped would possibly win another contest that would cover the remaining half of college, he thought he would just sleep during the day until he had to go into work. Tomorrow, he would take his piece over to Mike and have him edit it for him. When he walked over to the bed, he heard the phone ring at seven in the morning. He wondered who would be calling at this time of day. His dad has already left for work and his mom was still asleep. Steven thought it must be a wrong number, so he just let it ring until it stopped. As soon as it stopped, he went back to his bed, but again the phone rang. His mom still did not stir, so he decided to answer it because if they are calling back-to-back like this it must be important.

Steven answered the phone and heard Mike's mom over the phone.

"Steven, is this you?" Steven could tell that she sounded reserved and tired.

"Yeah, this is he, what's up?"

"Steven, I don't know how to tell you this." Steven heard Mike's mom crying over the phone, she kept crying and Steven didn't know why. His heart began to throb and he figured something must be wrong. "Ms. Adison, what's wrong, you're freaking me out." Steven's hands began to tremble.

"Steven, Mike passed away last night." Steven's eyes grew wide and he was in shock, so much so that his brain did not register what was said.

"What? WHAT?" Steven heard Ms. Adison crying again. Steven felt his world crash all around him.

"Ms. Adison, what do you mean Mike passed away?" After a period of silence, Ms. Adison finally broke the silence.

"Last night, Mike and I were coming home from school and we were involved in a car accident. As I was going through a green light, a delivery truck ran the red light and T-boned my car and it hit the passenger side where Mike was sitting." Steven heard her begin to sob over the phone. "He was killed instantly, I made it with some bruises, scrapes, and a broken arm, but Mike did not suffer, Steven, I promise." Steven's brain finally registered what had happened and Steven began to cry loudly, he fell to the ground, with the receiver in his hand and bawled. Elaine heard him and came into the kitchen and saw Steven crying on the phone. Steven was so hysterical, Elaine took the phone from his hand and spoke into it. What had happened was explained by Ms. Adison and Elaine hung up the phone and comforted her son.

The following Saturday was the day of the funeral for Mike. Steven felt so numb. Mike was his best friend; he was like a true brother to him. They spent so many nights together, writing sessions, playing video games, riding around the city with their bikes, and just talking about their hopes and dreams. Steven felt sick to his stomach, he has never attended a funeral before and when he woke up in the morning, he saw that it was a cool, October morning and raining. "Great, a typical funeral day." Steven got out of bed and got ready for the funeral.

Joe was at work, but Elaine told Steven she could drive him to the funeral if he wanted her too. Steven didn't want to drive; this whole week he did not want to do anything. He just wanted to sleep all day and do nothing. He had a hard time going to school and the whole week he missed work. His boss understood and told Steven he could take as much time off as he needed to recuperate from his loss.

They arrived at the funeral which was at the cemetery. Ms.

Adison wanted the funeral and burial held at the cemetery. Steven and Elaine got out of the car and there was a small crowd of about fifty people. Steven could tell half of it was extended family and students from school were the other half. Steven looked around to see where Ms. Adison was seated and he saw that she was surrounded by two men. One of them was Mike's biological dad, who was not much in Mike's life but at least had the decency to come to his own son's funeral. The other one was the man that she had been dating for the past several years and Mike liked him and thought of him as a father. Steven saw that her face was shrouded in sadness and her eyes were puffy; it looked like she had not stopped crying the whole week. She wore a black, short-sleeved dress and he saw that her left arm was in a cast and the other arm was bruised and covered with cuts that he knew must be from the shattered glass that poured in from Mike's window. Steven saw the casket and saw Mike's head lying in it—his face was covered in makeup from the mortician; they tried hard to cover up Mike's bruised and battered face, but underneath all of the makeup, Steven could see the lines where the cuts were from the glass and saw a large gash under his throat. Steven's heart sank. Did he really die instantly from the crash, or did he bleed to death from the throat? Steven would never find out, because soon after the funeral Ms. Adison moved to Florida, with her boyfriend to take a new job.

After the funeral, Ms. Adison walked up to Steven and gave him a hug. Before she left, she handed him a journal.

"Here Steven, I think this is something Mike would want you to have. It was the last thing he was working on." She handed him a leather notebook and Steven looked at it, with tears welling up in his eyes. He opened up the journal and saw the title, "Growing Up." He saw that it was similar to his own poem "Ballad of a Teenager," but this was more of a narrative and Steven saw that it was beautifully written. Steven looked up at Ms. Adison

"Thank you, I promise I will do everything I can to get this published under his own name."

Ms. Adison smiled, "Thank you, Steven, I know he would love to know you would do this for him."

Steven held the journal in his hands and saw that the clouds were clearing; he felt a warm breeze blow through his hair and he looked over at the casket. It looked as if Mike was gently smiling knowing that this work may possibly be published.

"Don't worry Mike, I promise to publish this in your honor and the money will go to your mom." Elaine walked up behind Steven and tapped him on the shoulder.

"You ready to go, honey?"

"Yeah, I am."

Two months passed since Mike's funeral and Steven devoted his spare time going through Mike's narrative and doing as much as he could to polish it as much as he could. He worked tirelessly to make sure that Mike's dream would come true. Steven knew that this piece was what Mike was working on to get into college. Mike's grades would have been only enough to cover a year of school and Mike must have been working on this to get a sizable scholarship to pay the remaining portion of it. Steven never once considered publishing this under his own name, he was already set for school. His other piece he sent won and now he did not have to worry about writing his own work until he started college next year. His priority was to get Mike's narrative published and give the proceeds to Ms. Adison.

It was winter break from school and Steven utilized his time to work on Mike's writing. Steven did pick up some extra hours at work and worked day shifts. Steven was saving the extra money for books and school supplies. He learned that his scholarship would only pay for school tuition and he wanted to save enough to pay for supplies and books so he did not have to work much while in college. He wanted to concentrate as much as he could on schoolwork.

When Steven was coming back from lunch break, he pulled into his work's parking lot. It was more of a dinner break, because he was working an evening shift. It was eight p.m. and it was dark outside. The moon was not out, so the night sky made the parking lot feel empty and lonely. When Steven got out of his car, his boss came running outside.

"Steven there you are, you need to get home now, something happened at home."

"What, what happened?"

"Your dad called and said he needed you to come home now, that is all he said."

"Okay, thanks." Steven jumped back into his car and sped off towards home.

When Steven got home, he saw several police cars and an

ambulance in front of his house.

"What the hell happened now?"

Steven figured it must have been his mom. He knew these past two years were too good to be true. But she seemed so normal lately, he did not expect anything from her. But then, he thought about his dad and his health.

"Oh, God, what if it's about him?"

He jumped out of the car and saw his dad on the front porch. His dad was covered in blood and his shirt was torn to shreds. The lights from the cars kept flashing against the light blue house and the moonless night made the night feel even more gloomy.

"Dad! Dad! What happened!"

Steven ran up the porch steps and approached his dad. He could see cut marks on his dad's face and that under the torn and tattered shirt there were cut marks all along his stomach. Steven could tell that his dad's belly looked bloated and swollen. The paramedics who were treating his dad turned around and told him to stay back.

"It's okay, it's my son."

"Okay, hurry up, we are going to need to take you to the hospital for an evaluation."

"Dad, what happened?"

Steven could tell his dad was breathing heavily and did not look good; not just from his injuries, but his body was swollen and he could tell that his dad's skin looked yellowish and his eyes looked red and swollen.

"Your mom attacked me while I was sleeping."

Steven's suspicions were half correct; it was about his mom

and his dad.

"She what?"

"I was sleeping and then I woke up with her clawing at me, scratching up my face and tearing up my shirt."

"Why?"

"I don't know, she was quiet the whole time; she just kept clawing at me with her nails, it looked like she grew out her nails for this purpose."

"Where is she anyways?"

"She's in her room; she locked herself in there and the police are trying to get her out. They are afraid to break in there because she may attack them."

"I don't blame them, if she did this to you with just her nails . . . I don't know what else she could do."

"Okay, Mr. Thomas," one of the paramedics stepped in, "We need to get you to the hospital to have you checked over."

"I don't want to go. It's just nail scratches."

"Well, honestly, we think you should be evaluated, okay."

Steven looked at the paramedics, he knew that they knew something was wrong with his dad besides the scratches; his skin color and swelling were not from the scratches, they suspected there was something else going on.

"Dad, I think you should go." Joe looked over at Steven.

"What, why?"

"Please dad, just go, okay?"

Steven's eyes grew watery, he knew that there is something going on with his dad. Joe looked at his son and realized that Steven really wanted him to go for his own sake.

"Okay, I'll go, but can I drive myself? I don't want to get

hit with an ambulance charge." The two paramedics looked at each other and shrugged.

"Yes, but we will follow you, we want to make sure that you make it to the hospital; we really think you should be evaluated."

"Okay, thanks."

"Thanks, Dad."

"Yeah, just stay here and watch over your mom and make sure that she gets help."

"Don't worry, I will." Joe went to his truck and drove off; the ambulance followed behind. Steven walked into the house and saw three cops standing by the bedroom door.

"Elaine, we need you to come out of the room or we will have to come in and get you." Steven walked up to the cops.

"Is she still in there?" One of the officers turned around and faced Steven.

"Are you the son?"

"Yes, can I try and help?"

"I don't know what good you can do; your mom has been in there for over an hour."

"Well, let me try to talk to her, okay?"

"Sure, go ahead." The officer's stepped aside and let Steven approach the door.

"Mom? It's me, Steven, will you please open the door."

Steven heard some rustling in the room, but she did not answer the door.

"I heard something," he whispered.

"Step back, I think she may be coming to the door."

"No, let us by it, you don't know what she will do."

"Well, as soon as the door opens, I will step aside and let you take over, okay?"

"Okay," one of the cops said.

"Mom, please open the door, you need help." Again, all Steven heard was some rustling from behind the door.

"Mom . . ." suddenly the door swung open and there was Elaine, with blood all over her hands. She stood there staring at Steven.

"I am so sorry" and then she fell onto her knees and began crying. Steven saw her put her hands against her face and saw that her nails were ripped down to the quick. He looked over at the bed and saw her nails lying on the top of the comforter. One of the cops gagged while another blurted out "She ripped off her nails to hide the evidence!" The third officer came to Elaine and picked her up. He turned her around and hand cuffed her and led her to one of the cop cars. "I'm sorry you had to see this, son," one of the officers told Steven.

"It's okay, I am used to this."

"Really?"

"Yeah, I have seen her numerous episodes; it's just this one came out of nowhere—she has been good for over two years." One of the officers overheard and Steven recognized him; he was one of the officers who has been here several times.

"Well, if what you say is true, it sounds like your mom's medication has been wearing off. We have seen this before; if they are on the same meds for too long, their body gets resistant over time. She probably just snapped."

Steven knew he was right; there were times where his mom grew resistant, but usually she had some warning signs before she got sick, plus this time she actually injured someone.

"Is she going to be arrested for assault?"

"Honestly, unless your dad presses charges, which he said he won't, she is going to be treated more for mental illness than arrested. We are just going to take her straight to the state hospital, don't worry, she'll get help."

"Okay, thank you."

Steven watched as his mom went into the cruiser and saw that she was still crying and saying, "I'm so sorry," over and over again. He saw the cruiser drive off and the third cop waved at Steven and told him "have a good night" and drove off behind the first car. Steven walked into the house and began to clean his mother's room. As he was cleaning, he took off the comforter and saw something catch his eye. His heart jumped into his throat and he saw a collection of steak knives, a carving knife, and two, large, butcher blades next to her pillow.

"Oh, my God, what if she decided to use these?"

Steven took the knives and threw them into the trash can in the back alley; he did not want his dad to ever know, because maybe his dad would change his mind about charging his mom. Steven went back into the house and cleaned up the rest of the bloody bedroom.

EPISODE NINE

Joe was in the hospital for a week; he was diagnosed with cirrhosis of the liver. The doctors told him that his liver was badly damaged and that he would likely never be able to get a liver transplant, due to it being caused by alcoholism. Something he was well aware of, this was the same situation with his brother, Christopher. The doctor, Dr. Challadra, was a nice, young doctor whose parents were from India but had moved to start a new life in America. Eventually, his parents had two children, and both went into med school. Dr. Challadra was very kind towards Joe and didn't treat Joe as a drunk, but as someone who suffered from depression and used alcohol as a form of anti-depressant.

"Mr. Thomas," Joe was expecting a thick accent from him but he did not know that he was a U.S. born citizen and had no trace of an accent.

"Your liver is over half-damaged, our only option besides a transplant is . . ." Joe looked at the doctor, whose dark brown eyes and black short hair accented his white uniform.

"I know, I know, I will never get a transplant, I will always be at the bottom of the donor list." Joe closed his eyes and sighed. "How long do I have?"

Dr. Challadra smiled. "It depends on how serious you are about quitting." Joe opened his eyes and looked over at the doctor; he could tell he was not kidding, his smile told all.

"You mean if I quit, I may live a full life?"

"No, not exactly, but you could get several years; your liver is damaged enough where it won't repair itself, but it isn't so far off that you cannot function at the state it is in." Joe sat up in his bed.

"If you completely quit, you may get another five to possibly ten years, you never know, the human body is capable of miraculous things."

Joe looked at him and stared; he knew it would be a hard battle to quit.

"But first we must get your swelling down because it is putting pressure on your limbs and heart; if we don't get it taken care of now, you will suffer some nerve damage to your limbs and possibly on your heart."

Joe sat there. Could he really quit? He never really tried to quit all together, sometimes he could get away with drinking less in a day, but never quit cold turkey without a drop.

"We will give you a variety of strong diuretics for several months; this will help bring down the swelling but also help with weight loss, having less weight will help overall." Joe did not like the sound of this.

"So, I am going to piss all the time?"

"At first, yes, but over time you will get to the point where you will just be going a lot at once rather than multiple times in the day."

"You really think I could live a few more years?"

"Yes, but you must never drink again, because if you ever get back into a cycle again you will destroy your liver even more."

"Do I need to wean off of it first, taper down?"

"No, you are starting now, and we will give you some medications for the withdrawals, because you will have intense headaches, cold sweats, and possibly seizures." Joe had a cold chill run down his spine, "seizures?"

"Possibly, not for certain, but based on how much you have consumed over your life and how dependent your body is on it, you may get seizures. But don't worry, again, I will prescribe medication for it as a PRN—meaning you only have to take it if you have one and then call us to let us know."

Joe sat there amazed; he could live a little longer, his brother had this same chance but he kept drinking. Joe could have had his older brother a little longer, if he had followed the directions. He was going to do it; his son was going to graduate in six months and will be going to college. He never told his son how proud he was of him. He may have yelled at him, been angry at him for petty things, but he really was proud of his son and how far he has come with his writing. The rest of the week in the hospital, Joe ruminated over how he will be different towards Elaine and Steven.

After Joe was released from the hospital, Steven took the news pretty hard. During his dad's stay in the hospital, he stayed home and took care of the house, since his mom was gone too. It felt odd to Steven to have the house to himself for a week, but he was too afraid to go see his dad. He wanted to keep his mind off things by staying home and taking care of the house—cleaning, cooking for himself, and working on Mike's narrative. When Joe returned, Steven saw how much weight his dad had already lost. He was only gone a week but when Joe walked into the living room, as Steven was finishing up eating, he saw that his dad's limbs were getting smaller and that his belly looked less bloated, even his face seemed narrower now. He got up and ran to his dad and gave him a hug. Joe told him everything.

"Don't worry, Dad, I will make sure you quit."

"Well, I already have," Joe smiled at Steven.

"Well, you know what I mean, I will make sure you stay sober, okay?" Steven ran into the kitchen and began pouring out all of the liquor and beer in the house.

"I am starting now," he said from the kitchen. Joe could hear the cans of beer opening; he wanted one so badly, but he really wanted to quit, no matter how badly the urge was nagging him.

"Thank you, Steven, I honestly don't know if I could have done it myself." Joe walked to the couch and turned on the news. He sat there thankful that he did not lose his job, his bosses were very supportive and, in fact, happy that he was going to hopefully quit drinking. Even though his drinking did not affect his work directly, they did notice how he was slowing down and that his health was deteriorating. Joe would go back to work in one more week, they wanted to make sure he was well enough to go back.

"By the way, Dad, have you eaten anything yet?" Steven walked out of the kitchen and saw his dad sitting on the couch.

"No, I'll just make a sandwich later, I'm really not that hungry right now."

"Okay, well if you need anything let me know, I start back school from winter break in a couple days, I can help out if you need me too?"

"Thanks Steven, but I will be okay, I do already feel much better, still a little tired, but if I feel this good in one week, I could only imagine what I will feel like in another week." Joe smiled at Steven and then laid down on the couch. Steven knew to leave his dad alone, he still needed to rest.

Steven went in his room and sat at his desk. He just sat there in thought; he could tell he was slowly slipping into a depression. He felt so tired even with just that forty-five-minute confrontation with his dad. Deep down, he felt happy to know that as long as his dad stayed sober, he had some more life to live, but Steven's past was catching up to him, and so were his nightmares. Everything that had happened the past several years would replay in his dreams and now they were creeping up on him in the daytime. He could not stop thinking about his grandma's death and never being able to go to her funeral; he still felt hurt from Mike's unexpected death. Working on Mike's story was a double-edged sword; on one hand, he felt honored to complete his dead best friend's last work but working on it meant that it constantly reminded Steven of how much he missed Mike. Not only that, it showed how lonely he was without Mike.

Mike was his only and best friend; they did everything

together. They did make some minor friends along the way in high school, but never close enough to spill his guts to, like he could with Mike. At this point, Steven just hoped he could maybe make a friend in college. It was his senior year in high school and felt it was pointless to make a friend that would probably more than likely move away or go to a different college. Steven just sat there and closed his eyes and sighed. Then he decided to work on Mike's narrative a little more.

Soon May arrived and it was near graduation for Steven. Elaine made it out of the hospital a month earlier, just in time to see her son graduate from high school. Joe's appearance was drastically changed compared to what he looked like back in December. Joe's complexion even changed, and his skin seemed to smooth out. Joe was slender and some of his muscles were showing in his arms. He was not muscular and heavily built, but he was slender enough where his muscles would slightly show. Joe was also more energetic and seemed happy. He was more jovial and joked around a lot with Steven and when Elaine got out of the hospital, Joe helped out by cleaning the house and even cooked. Steven almost fell down in astonishment to see his dad cook one day when Elaine got home. It wasn't the greatest tasting meal, but it was still good to Steven. Even though his dad worked in restaurants, he had to remind himself that his dad managed the cooks, not cooked himself.

The biggest thing that Steven felt he had accomplished was that during spring break, he completed Mike's narrative and sent it off to some publishers. Recently, one called back and offered to publish it. They asked Steven if he would like to have his name on it or to receive the advance and future royalties, but he declined and gave Ms. Adison's information and told them that it was Mike's mother and that she deserved the money. Steven did not know where she lived in Florida, but he did find out that the publisher located her and was able to successfully get the money sent to her. The next day Ms. Adison called.

Steven was getting ready for the last Monday of his high school career when he heard the phone ring. He went to answer it and was surprised to hear Ms. Adison's voice on the other end of the line.

"Hello, is this Steven?" He could hear her crying, but it sounded like tears of joy rather than sorrow.

"Yes, this is he, is this Ms. Adison?"

"Yes, it is, I am calling to thank you so much for what you did for Mike." Steven smiled with tears welling in his eyes out of joy.

"You are welcome, it was the least I could do for him; he helped me out so much."

"I know, and he spoke so highly of you, Steven. Steven, you did not have to give me the money, you could have kept it."

"No, it would not be right, you deserve that money; he was your son." There was a long silence.

"Steven, can I at least give you half of the advancement money?" Steven was surprised. He honestly did not do this for the money, he really wanted Mike's mom to get all the money.

"No, I could not accept any of it, really."

"Please, Steven, it's the least I can do for you." Steven stood there, with the phone in his hands. He really did not want the money; it would not feel right. He did not want Ms. Adison to think that this was his plan; he really did this all for Mike's honor and his wishes.

"Please, Steven," he could hear Ms. Adison sob over the phone. "I am well off, and I am about to get remarried. Don't worry, it's with the same guy I have been with; Mike really liked him and if Mike liked him, then I know he must be a good guy." Steven heard a soft chuckle from her, Mike was good at picking out good people.

"Please Ms. Adison, I don't know if I could." She broke in quickly.

"Steven, in my heart I think Mike would like you to have part of this money. He knew how important it was for both of you to go to school and he knew how much you want to be an author. I know you have a full scholarship for school and that it does not cover books or supplies. Giving you half of Mike's advance, I think will help you concentrate on school. If my son will not be able to go to school, please do it for me. You finishing school will be like knowing Mike did, please take half of it."

Steven was shocked, even with half of the advance, it was still a sizable sum. Not only would he be able to pay supplies and books, but he would be able to only work two days a week and still get by well enough.

"Okay, I will accept it."

"Thank you, Steven, this makes me feel so much better." He could tell she was sincere about it. Steven wanted to ask her about the cut under Mike's throat, but decided it was not a good time.

Graduation day finally arrived and it was a warm and beautiful, late May morning. Greenery was in full force and all the trees were in full bloom and it felt more like the beginning of summer than late spring. Joe was dressed up and so was Elaine. Joe never took a day off from work, unless he was sick, but today he took it off for his son. He was very proud of Steven and even more proud knowing that Steven would be the first one in his family to go off to college. He was even more proud of his son for getting a full ride for school and how hard he had worked to get that. Joe even wrote a card for Steven and was going to give it to him after graduation. Elaine was getting ready and Steven could hear her softly crying. He walked into her room and asked her what was wrong.

"Mom, are you okay?" Elaine wiped her eyes with the palms of her hands and turned around.

"Honestly, no. After you graduate, you are going to leave me." She turned around and hugged Steven tightly.

"What do you mean, I'm not going to leave you." He could hear her sniffling; he hoped her snot would not get on his button down shirt.

"You are going to pick a college and I know you won't do the one here in Topeka." Steven stood there, he considered going to Washburn, but he wanted to go to Wichita State.

"Mom, even if I went to a different college, I would still visit."

"Yeah, but I know I haven't been in your life as much as you liked; I want to be in it more." Steven's heart sank, he loved his mom, but at the same time he thought if he went to another college out of town, his nightmares might decrease.

"We will see, Mom, okay, I have not decided for sure."

"I know, I am sorry." As Steven walked out of the room, he saw that her pill bottles were empty.

At the graduation ceremony, Steven talked to his dad away from his mom.

"Hey, Dad, I was in mom's room earlier today and saw that she had some empty pill bottles."

"Yeah, I know, she said she had just run out today; we will pick up her refills after this." Steven sighed in relief.

"Okay, good, was just making sure."

"I know, I thought the same thing. Anyways, the ceremony is about to start, you should probably line up with your class." Steven hugged his dad and ran off to meet his classmates.

During the ceremony, Elaine cried the whole time.

"Elaine, what's wrong?"

"Steven is going to leave us." Joe held her hand, and Steven looked into the crowd and saw his dad holding his mom's hand. Steven smiled. He had never seen his dad hold his mom's hand before; he could not even remember if he ever saw them kiss before. Steven was proud of his dad for being sober; he could tell how his dad's mood had changed so much. His dad not only seemed happier, but he was more affectionate towards him and his mom. He could not remember the last time his dad yelled at them.

As Steven was staring off into the crowd, he heard his name ring out over the speakers. "Steven Thomas." Steven looked over and saw a gap in front of him, he blushed and then proceeded to walk across the stage. He heard his dad clapping and cheering and saw that his mom was still crying. Steven grabbed his certificate and waved at the crowd. He then went and sat down in the assigned seats and listened to the upcoming speech.

After the ceremony, Steven found his parents and his dad handed him an envelope.

"What's this?" he looked at his dad in confusion, he had never received a card from his dad before.

"Open it."

He saw his dad smirking. Steven was not expecting money. He knew, since he worked and had his own source of income, his parents did not give him any money, plus his parents did not have much extra money to spare anyways. Steven opened it and saw that his dad had written him a note:

> *Dear Steven, I know we have not been close when you were growing up, and I know I don't say it often but I am very proud of you son and that I love you very much. You have become an outstanding young man and I am so happy to see how hard you worked to get yourself a full ride to college. I just wanted you to know that I do love you and that I am very proud of you Steven.*
> *Love, Dad*

Steven teared up and looked at his father. He could tell his dad was tearing up too and smiled. Steven walked towards his dad and gave him a big hug.

"Thanks, Dad."

"You're welcome, Steven." Elaine just stood there sobbing,

"He's going to leave us." And then she took some tissues out of her purse and dabbed her eyes.

It was mid-June and Steven had not selected the college he would be attending. His top choice was Wichita, but he did not know if he was willing to go to school away from home. He wanted to get out of Topeka badly, mainly because he felt that if he lived in a different city that his nightmares would decrease, and that being away from the city where all his bad memories originated would help his depression.

Today was the day he would be going on a tour at Wichita State to see for sure if he wanted to attend. He heard that it had a great English and writing program and that was another reason why he wanted to go there. Steven was getting ready when he noticed his mom lying in bed sobbing.

"Mom, are you okay?" She just laid there sobbing, not saying anything to Steven. He felt bad, he knew that she knew that he was going to visit Wichita State today and she is taking it pretty hard.

"Mom, don't worry, I don't know for sure if I will go there, I just want to check it out to make sure." His mom turned around and looked at him, he could tell that she must have been crying all night. He felt guilty, but he wanted to choose the school he felt was best for him.

"Well, I'm going to go now, I'll be back home before four." She did not reply, she just turned back over and got back under the covers. Steven sighed and got into his car.

When Steven finally arrived at Wichita State, he instantly fell in love with the school. It sat on a large campus and he saw the mix of old buildings from when the school was built combined with some of the newer ones that were recently added. He looked over and saw the mascot, a scarecrow with wheat in his mouth, in yellow and black staring at him from the center of the campus. Steven saw that there was a large courtyard and several walking paths that snaked around the campus. He saw that it was close to downtown. He loved all the different shops and how everything was so condensed in a city with a metro of over half a million. He loved how the river snaked next to downtown and that there was a beautiful river walk that traversed across the city. Steven could see himself sitting along the banks and writing while watching the sun rise and set. He breathed in and felt that this would be a great new start for his life.

Steven met with the coordinator and was shown around the campus. He listened to the rehearsed lecture that she probably went through hundreds of times. But he did not care, he just loved the new setting and tone of the city. It felt fresh and new and the city felt abuzz. Even during the summer, the school seemed abuzz with activity, summer classes were being held and there were other possible students touring the school as well. Steven smiled and made up his mind, he knew this is where he wanted to attend.

Steven headed home; he did not sign any paperwork just yet, he wanted to talk it over with his mom first and try to soften the blow. He knew his dad did not mind; his dad was just happy that he was going to go attend college. He knew his dad preferred that he attend Washburn like his mother, but Joe wanted his son to be happy at whichever school he preferred. Steven pulled up to the house and looked at his watch. It was three thirty, a little sooner than he expected. His dad's truck was still gone, and his mom's car was still in the parking lot.

Steven walked into the house and saw his mom sitting on the couch with the TV off.

"Hey, Mom, I think I decided where I would like to go." Steven walked next to his mom and sat on the couch besides her. He looked at her and she did not say a word. He could tell that her eyes were still puffy from her tears.

"Mom, did you hear me?" Elaine just stared off into the distance. Steven waved his hand in front of her and noticed that she did not blink; she just stood there like a statue, lightly breathing, and staring off into space. Steven knew that this must be a start of an episode. He got up quickly, but as soon as he did, his mom grabbed him by his wrist.

"You will not take my boy away from me again." Steven's eyes grew wide and he began to panic.

"Oh no, she must think I am a demon again." Steven tried to break free from her tight grasp, but he could not get free. Even though his mom was now close to fifty, she still had tremendous strength. He could feel her nails digging into his wrist.

"Mom, it's me Steven!"

"No, you are the devil, you are trying to take him away from me." Steven saw her free hand shift and grab something from underneath the cushion; then he saw the sunlight from the window reflect off the silver blade.

Steven began to panic; he could not break free from his mom. He saw the large butcher knife glistening in his mom's left hand.

"Mom, Mom, it's me Steven, I am not the devil!"

"Lier!" She plunged the knife towards Steven and with his free hand, he grabbed his mom's hand by her wrist, fighting to keep it from getting close to him. They were locked, a hand on each other's wrist, Steven fighting to keep the blade from touching his throat. Suddenly, a flash of Mike's own throat flashed before his eyes.

"No!" Steven used his full force to shift the knife hand away and pushed his mom back, this sudden movement dazed her enough to weaken her grasp and Steven finally broke free. Steven had to think fast; his first thought was to call the police, but he knew he could not do it fast enough—his mom would catch up to him again. His only chance was to get out of the house and get next door.

"I almost had you, Satan, but I'll get you again." Elaine ran towards the knife. Steven felt stupid, he should have grabbed it as soon as he was free. Elaine got to it and ran towards Steven swiftly. Steven could still not believe how fast and agile his mom was for her age. Steven turned around and ran towards the kitchen to get out but saw that his mom had boarded the entryway.

"What the hell?" And then, there he was, trapped in the kitchen; his mom was blocking the entryway to the kitchen and now he was stuck. He would not be able to get out the back door and now his mom was blocking the only way out.

"I have you now!" Elaine stood there and Steven could see that his mom's eyes were empty. It seemed as if there was no soul behind those eyes. They burned with an intense fire but behind that fire there was nothing—nothing was behind those eyes. Steven began to breathe heavily and he was afraid for his life. He did not know what to do; he would not be able to get past his mom, with a large knife in her hand. He looked around the kitchen, and then saw the kitchen table.

Steven ran behind the table and then pushed it towards his mom. She fell with a large thud and the knife fell out of her hand. "Now's my chance." Steven crawled over the table and jumped over his mom; as soon as he landed on his feet, he tripped. His mom got ahold of his right ankle and held on to it. Steven saw that the knife was still lying about two feet away and he began to shift his body around to go grab it. Elaine saw what he was doing and swung her right hand around to catch it. Steven was too late. Elaine grabbed the knife and then crawled on top of Steven.

"I've got you now, years of torment are now over!" She took both of her hands and grasped the knife with both of them and plunged it towards Steven.

Steven grabbed her wrists, with both of his hands, and fought her off as best as he could. He could not break free from beneath her; her weight was still greater than his. He was tall and lanky, but his mom was tall and heavy; he could not get out from underneath her. Steven then began screaming "Help! Help!" hoping that maybe someone would hear him. He kept yelling but no one came. Steven began to cry and did not know what to do. He was going to die and by his own mother, but then it hit him—it was not his mom, it was someone else. He knew his mom would never really kill him, but whoever this was, wanted him dead, because they thought he was the devil. With tears running down his cheeks, Steven yelled out.

"You are not my mother. You have never been my mom!" As soon as these words were spoken, Steven felt the strength behind his mom slowly fade away. He looked into his mom's eyes and saw that they were glossed over. His mom was in there somewhere and heard what he said. Steven saw the flame behind the eyes slowly burn out and it looked like his mom was in there somewhere. Elaine dropped the knife and began to cry.

"Mom? Mom?" Elaine looked between her fingers and softly said,

"Steven?"

"Yes, Mom, it is me." Steven was shocked, was his mom back to normal, or was she still delusional.

"Steven? You're going to leave me!" Elaine began to cry. "I don't feel so good, Steven, I need help."

"I know, Mom, I know, let's go." Steven stood and picked his mom up. He felt so guilty for what he said, his mom did not seem to be there, but after what he said, her whole demeanor changed, he knew his mom deep down heard what he said.

"Mom, let me help you into the car." He opened the door for his mother and helped her get situated in the seat. She was still crying, her hair was covered in sweat and matted across her face. Her hands were trembling.

"Steven, are you going to leave me?"

Steven looked at his mom. "No, Mom, I decided I will be going to Washburn."

Elaine looked up at him and wiped away her tears. Steven then started the car and drove off to get help for his mom.

EPISODE TEN

Three years passed, Steven turned twenty-one and a lot had happened since he started college at Washburn. It may have not been his number one choice, but they did have a respectable English degree; he was a little disappointed to learn that they did not offer a creative writing program or at least an emphasis in creative writing. But he was okay with it, because he knew that an English degree was still good enough to pursue an MFA when he was finished with his undergraduate degree.

One of the changes was his home life. His dad told Steven that he could still live at home to save money and not have to spend money on a dorm, since the college was in the middle of the city. Steven was very grateful, because with the extra money he saved up from working, along with the advancement that Ms. Adison let him keep, he had enough money to take off from work, until he finished his degree, in which he was only one year away. His family life was pretty stable. Elaine had not had an episode since the last one and luckily it was deemed a smaller one, since she got better fairly quickly. She was only in the hospital for a month and did not have to go to a rehabilitation home; she came home and acted like nothing even happened, which was usual for her.

Steven did notice that his father was acting a little different. Joe seemed more reserved and not as jovial as he was after he first became sober. He seemed more irritated, he did not get into fights with Elaine or Steven, but Steven could tell that his father was different the last three or four years since he was diagnosed with cirrhosis of the liver. Also, Joe demoted himself to an assistant manager position that let him work fewer hours and spend more time at home which Steven thought was a big surprise. It seemed that working the long hours actually helped keep him sober; it seemed to keep his dad's mind off of things.

When Steven turned twenty-one, he did not go out and party. Steven saw what alcohol did to his family and seeing it close to home with his father hit him hard enough to prevent an interest in drinking. Sometimes, Steven was tempted to try it just to see how he liked it, he even thought that maybe having a few drinks would help with his still constant nightmares. His nightmares still happened on a nightly basis and he knew his depression was growing ever deeper, except that the new and biggest thing that happened in his life did manage to help a little bit.

After about a year in college, Steven met his current girlfriend, just turned fiancé. Her name was Marie Williams and Steven loved her dearly. Marie was about three years older than Steven and graduated as a RN. They met in freshman composition, she was a junior and pushed it off till her next to last year. When Steven walked into the room, he saw her, with her beautiful, curly, brown hair and deep blue eyes. She was sitting at the back of the class and seemed reserved. Steven decided to sit next to her but he was too afraid to say hello.

One day, after about a couple of weeks into the class, Steven was working on some poems and dropped one of them onto the floor. Marie saw that it slid under her desk and picked it up. Steven never wrote love poetry but the poem he was working on that she managed to pick up was about her, not directly, but the title was "Sapphire Eyes" and he was afraid that she would see that it was about her.

"Hey, you dropped this." She handed him the piece of paper, smiling beautifully at Steven. He could see that she had perfectly straight teeth that were pearly white; it matched her soft, ivory skin.

"Oh, thank you." He blushed and grabbed the paper and tucked it underneath his folder. "I like the title." Steven's hair stood up on end.

Oh no, did she read it? She seemed to have held onto it for a few seconds; maybe the title is all she got. He began to panic and wanted to get up and use the bathroom as a way to break this up.

"It sounds beautiful, maybe one of these days I can read it." Steven stood still, did she or did she not read it? Was she being nice and playing it off? Steven did not know.

"Uh, yeah. Maybe after I finish editing it." Steven sat there looking at her smiling back at him.

"Uh hmm," Dr. Bird was dry coughing. "As I was saying," he looked at both Steven and Marie.

"Sorry" they said in unison, both blushing. They looked

back up front to listen to the rest of the lecture.

After the lecture that evening, Steven walked out and saw the sun setting off on the horizon. He loved that in college that you could pick numerous classes, during such a broad amount of time. He enjoyed taking evening classes, because he was such a night owl. Steven did most of his writing over the night and would go to bed late in the early morning at around two or three a.m. Plus, with his nightmares that would wake him up, he could sleep in till past noon until he had to go to his afternoon classes. It was a good balance to keep him awake enough for school but being able to live with the fact that the nightmares would wake him up constantly.

Steven was walking and felt the cool, fall breeze brush through his hair. Then he felt a tap on his shoulder and turned around. He saw Marie standing there and he did not realize how short she was compared to him. Her head reached to the bottom of his chin, but she was even more beautiful to him now.

"Hey, so when do you think I can read that poem?" she gave him a wink.

"Well, I have to edit it and stuff."

"I know silly, I knew that. You never had someone ask you out on a date before, have you?" she was lightly laughing. Steven stared at her—a date? He had never had a date before; he never even dared to ask a girl out. Sure, he had some crushes, but he never dared ask a girl out; he was too afraid of rejection.

"Um, honestly, no, I've never even had a girlfriend before." Steven looked down and blushed from ear to ear. What the hell did he just say, he felt embarrassed, how could he say that to her.

"Oh, it's okay" she began to laugh. She looked up at him.

"Oh, I'm sorry, I didn't mean to make you feel uncomfortable." Steven looked back at her and saw her eyes twinkle from the sun behind him—her eyes really did sparkle like blue sapphires. Steven cleared his throat.

"Well, I like to drink coffee, would you like to meet at a coffee shop some time?"

"Sure, how about this Saturday. I'm off work on the weekends. I work over nights as a CNA; I am currently working on my RN degree right now."

"I don't work, so any day works for me." What did he just say? Great, now she is going to think he was a bum.

"Well, I mean I did work, but I made some money off my writing, and have a full ride for school, so I can concentrate on my degree. I want to get my MFA, so I can enhance my craft and teach at the college level."

"Oh, wow, that sounds so cool." Steven looked at her and smiled.

"I can tell you more at the coffee shop this weekend."

"Great, sounds like a date." She smiled at him and walked away. Steven's heart felt warm; he did not realize it but he was smiling ear to ear. At a distance, he could hear her yell across the parking lot.

"By the way, don't forget your poem," then she got in her car and drove off.

Steven and Marie met at the local coffee shop, the Black Bird Roast House. Steven always enjoyed going there and he was a local favorite at the shop. He did many open mic nights there and was well received. He walked into the shop and saw Tommy at the counter.

"Hey, Steven, the usual?" Steven always got the almond milk iced latte, with almond flavoring; he never got anything else.

"You know it." Steven sat down at his usual spot back in the far corner of the shop and began editing "Blue Sapphires." He felt that if Marie was going to read it eventually, it might as well be now. Steven worked on his piece, until Tommy brought him his drink.

"Here you go."

"Thanks."

"What are you working on now? Are you thinking of reading that tonight?" Steven looked up at him; he forgot that this Saturday was the last Saturday of the month and it was poetry reading night.

"Uh, honestly, I forgot, I was working on this for someone."

"Oh, I see, you are doing commissions now." Tommy laughed, his long, brown hair bouncing with his diaphragm. Steven looked at him.

"I'm only kidding."

"Well, it's actually for a girl I met in my class; I dropped it and she picked it up and saw the title and she wanted to read it."

"Oh, sweet, you got a date then?" As soon as Tommy said that, Marie walked into the shop. She saw Steven sitting in the back and walked towards him. Tommy saw her and bent down and whispered in Steven's ears. "Boy, she is good looking."

"Shut up," Steven lightly replied.

Marie walked up towards Steven.

"Is this seat taken?" she laughed. Steven smiled.

"Yes, for a nice girl in my class." Marie chuckled.

"Cute, and polite." Steven's heart raced, she called him cute? Tommy stepped in. "Welcome to Black Bird, can I grab you something." Marie looked up.

"Sure, I'll take a coffee, black, with some cream and sugar on the side."

"Sure thing, I'll be right back." Tommy walked back behind the counter and got her drink. He walked back over with the order and laid it on the table. As she was getting into her purse, Steven held his hand out.

"I'll pay for it."

"Oh, you don't have to."

"No, I insist." Steven got out his wallet and gave Tommy a five and told him to keep the rest.

"Thanks, Steven," and then Tommy walked back behind the counter.

"Well, I gave you a few days to edit your poem, you have it finished yet?" Marie took a quiet sip from her coffee; the steam was rising above her brown hair.

"Yeah, it's about done."

"When can I read it?"

"I don't know; I don't have all the kinks worked out yet. I tried to get here a little early to finish up, but I came late."

"It's okay, I can read what you have so far." Steven blushed lightly, he was nervous, he did not want her to read it yet. As he was sitting there a regular, Liam, walked through the door. He saw Steven sitting in the back.

"Hey Steven, you going to read tonight?" Steven looked up at Liam. He was a nice guy, a fellow English major in Steven's graduating class. He was tall and lanky and always talked quickly, as if he was always happy and excited.

"Well, um, I forgot today was open reading night."

"Forgot? You always come here to read your works." Marie looked over at Steven.

"Hey, maybe you can read 'Blue Sapphires' tonight." Steven felt crushed. Now not only will she finally hear it, it will also be told to everyone in the coffee shop.

"Blue Sapphires?" Liam looked at the paper on the table.

"Oh, I knew you were just playing dumb, you were working on a piece for tonight." Steven sat there quietly. "Well, I look forward to hearing it tonight; I heard the last piece you read was accepted last week. It was in the 'what's happening now with our majors' email." Marie looked over at Steven.

"Wow, you really are a famous writer."

"I'm not famous, I just have some works published."

"Yeah, and some that were great enough to land you a full ride to school," Liam was laughing. "Well, I'll catch you later, Steven, I look forward hearing your piece tonight."

Marie and Steven sat there talking and Steven learned more about her. He could tell that she loved and cared for people and that her becoming a nurse was a profession that suited her well. She kept looking into Stevens eyes and smiling at him.

"You know, ever since the first day of class, I thought you were really cute, Steven." She blushed and took her last sip of her coffee. Steven did not know what to say. "And I can tell that you have a very gentle soul. The way you carry yourself in class, you seem to have a mature nature, even though you are a few years younger than me." Steven looked up at her in surprise. "I graduate next year and pushed off freshman comps till this semester; I'll be taking senior comp next semester—English class has never been my forte." She laughed and stuck her hand out and placed it onto Steven's. Steven looked down and saw her painted purple nails. She was gently caressing the top of his hand.

"Yeah, I have lived a pretty extraordinary life." He did not think this was the right time to tell her about his past, but he felt he should; if he told her now, at least she could decide as to whether or not she would want to see him anymore, so he told her about his past. After about half an hour, Marie simply smiled and said, "Good thing my specialty is going to be in psyche." Steven knew at that moment he would read "Blue Sapphires" tonight.

It was two years ago when Steven read "Blue Sapphires" and Marie knew it was about her; she thought it was the sweetest gesture any person could ever do. Since then, they were inseparable. Marie loved both of Steven's parents and never thought any less of either of them. Steven knew she was the one and proposed to her on the anniversary of Steven reading the poem that was dedicated to her. Steven and Marie spent the last month planning for their wedding and Steven hoped his dad would be well enough to attend, let alone attend his graduation, since he would be graduating just one month before their wedding day.

It was after Christmas and Steven came home for the holidays from visiting Marie's parents. Steven walked into the living room and smelled something off in the house. It smelled as if the air was rancid and something was decaying. He looked over at his father and saw him lying on the couch. Steven's heart sank and saw that his dad's skin was yellow and that his eyes were the same color. Elaine came out of the kitchen with a bowl of soup.

"Mom, what's wrong with dad?" Elaine set the bowl on the coffee table and walked up to Steven.

"Your dad has not been feeling well the past few days." Steven looked at his dad.

"I was only gone since the twenty-sixth." He looked over at his father who began to moan. Elaine walked over and helped him sit up. She held the bowl to him.

"Here, Joe, you need to eat a little something." Joe held the bowl and just stared into it. Elaine got back up and talked to Steven.

"Your father has not eaten anything since you and Marie were here for Christmas." Steven thought about it and realized that his father did not eat much on Christmas day. He started to think more and thought how his dad's skin did seem to be changing color. But being around it every day, it's not as noticeable. But being away three days straight and now coming home, it was obvious.

"Did dad go see the doctor recently?" Steven looked over at his dad who just sat there staring into the bowl of soup.

"Yes," and Elaine paused.

"What?" Steven looked at his mom who he saw was tearing up. "He went the day you went to Marie's parent's house for the three days and he was told that his liver is almost completely damaged." Steven felt the floor release from beneath him, he could not stand up without having to lean against the door.

"What does that mean?" He looked at his mom's blue eyes that were covered in a thick layer of tears.

"I don't know, Steven, but it looks like not too long off." Steven began to tremble.

"Why is he not at the hospital? Can't they help?"

"Your dad did not want to stay; he said if he is going to go, he rather do it here, and kept insisting that he did not want to rack up a hospital bill for us to take care of."

Steven didn't know what to do, he looked at his father and wanted to say something, but he could tell that his dad did not feel well and looked like he did not want to be bothered. He hugged his mom silently and went and called Marie. Steven told her what was going on.

Marie arrived shortly afterwards and walked into the house. The smell of decay was strong in the house. She saw Joe laying in the couch with his eyes closed; it looked like he was having trouble breathing. She saw his skin and it looked greenish-yellow and he looked wet from perspiration. "Oh, God, Steven, I am so sorry," Marie ran to Steven and hugged him.

Marie had been working as an ER nurse for the last

year. She usually gets the patients that come in with mental health history, and evaluates them before they are sent to the behavioral health facility that is part of the hospital network that she works in.

"Steven, I hate to tell you this, but your dad is not too far off." Steven began to tear up and closed his eyes.

"Should we take him to the hospital; my mom said he does not want to go, but I think he should." Marie looked over at Joe and teared up. She has seen this several times at the emergency room. She shook her head.

"At this point, there is nothing to do, I am pretty sure his organs are" . . . and suddenly Joe rolled over and threw up all over the floor. It was all blood.

Steven's eyes opened wide and he almost fainted; his dad began coughing and gagging. All Joe said was "Oh, God!" and then he would throw up blood and bile. Marie rushed into the kitchen and grabbed a trash can and placed it under Joe.

"Joe, we need to go to the hospital now!" Steven was in shock; he did not know what to do. Elaine was crying and was frantic.

"Marie, Marie, is there anything I can do to help." Elaine didn't know if she could really help, but she felt she needed to do something.

Suddenly, Joe stopped throwing up and looked up at Steven and said, "Sorry," and then he went into convulsions. He rolled onto his back and began to stare at the ceiling while rapidly breathing and locking his legs and arms.

"Elaine, he's beginning to seize, call help now!" Elaine ran to the kitchen and called for the ambulance.

The whole time Steven was in shock. The blood was everywhere and it was all over the carpet, on the base of the couch, and running down the coffee table. The smell was rancid, a mix of foul bile and blood mixed with decaying flesh. Steven grew sick to his stomach; he ran outside to get some air. Then he heard the sound of sirens off in the distance. To his surprise, he saw two fire trucks and an ambulance pull up. Two people came from each truck and soon six people rushed past Steven; he turned around and went back inside.

When he came in, Marie stepped away and one of the paramedics asked a fireman to help Joe onto the living room floor.

"We need him on a hard surface fast; we need to put a tube in him to breathe. It looks like he had a massive coronary!" The two men took Joe and laid him on the floor. He was still staring off into space, rapidly breathing, Steven could only describe the sound as a death rattle; it was as if his father was hyperventilating but with a blood curdling rattle in between. A female paramedic rushed over with a needle and tried getting it into his father. But as soon as the needle pierced the skin in his abdomen, a long line of blood gushed forth and landed two feet away, landing on Steven's shoes. One of the paramedics came up to Steven. "Son, you should not see this, you need to go outside." Steven stood there in shock, he could not move, then Marie came up to him and got in his face.

"Steven, honey, you need to leave the house; you should not see this." Steven snapped out of it when he saw his future wife's face. He nodded and walked out of the house into the biting, cold January night.

Steven paced back and forth crying, hoping a miracle would happen. Soon the paramedics and firemen came outside with the stretcher and loaded his father into the back of the ambulance; in the corner of his eye, Steven could still see his dad convulsing.

"Steven, get in my car, your mom can sit in the back, we'll meet them at the hospital." Steven numbly walked to the passenger side and the whole way there, they trailed the ambulance and the sound of sirens echoed through the night.

When they got to the hospital, Marie led Steven and Elaine into where she knew Joe would end up. He was immediately sent to the back of the emergency room, where the critical care unit would step in. Steven wanted to see his father but one of the nurses closed the blinds and stepped out into the hallway.

"Not right now, the doctors are going to look at him now." Steven understood and stood there looking at the blinds, hoping that maybe he could catch a glimpse of his father on the other side.

"Steven, let's go to the waiting room, they will update us there, I don't think you want to see what's in there anyway." The three went to a private waiting room and waited. Steven could not sit, he just walked back and forth, many things rushed through his head. Above all else, he felt guilty. He knew his dad did not look too good, but he still went to Marie's parents anyway. He felt selfish, he should have been there to help with his dad, he should have done something, he felt helpless.

After a long hour passed, the doctor finally came in. He had some blood on his gown and he walked in shaking his head.

"Which one of you is Steven?" Steven looked at him.

"I'm Steven." He said hoarsely.

"Oh, you are next to kin then?" Steven looked at him.

"Sorry, but your dad is in very bad shape. You see, your dad had a massive coronary and we ran some more tests and his liver is entirely destroyed—it is barely even functioning. From the time the seizure happened until his arrival, which was about twenty-five minutes, he had no oxygen to his brain. He is brain dead and his liver is gone. Even if he managed to get a transplant, he would have to ride a helicopter to Kansas City, since we do not specialize in liver transplants. Now, he would more than likely not survive the ride alone. And then if he did get a transplant, he has a one percent survival rate. If he did manage to survive the transplant, he lost so much oxygen to his brain that he would be brain dead the rest of his life, plus the heart is severely damaged." The doctor paused and looked at Steven.

"Since your mother and father were not married, you have the legal say on what to do with your father." Steven looked at the doctor confused. "Son, your dad is on life support, and in my medical opinion, he is almost dead. He is only breathing thanks to the tube, if the tube was taken out, he would pass in minutes, which is why he would not be able to survive the ride to Kansas City, the helicopter cannot support the machine." Steven for the first time, since the car ride there, sat down. He looked at the floor, he could not cry, he had a hard time comprehending what was being said. "Steven, you have a decision to make." The doctor looked at him sternly. Marie walked over to Steven and held his hand and kissed it. Steven knew what needed to be done.

"Okay, do it."

"Just to let you know, this is the best decision for your father. If you want, you can come see him before we take him off." Steven looked at the doctor and slowly got up and followed him.

Steven walked into the room and saw his dad laying there connected to tubes, wires, and so many machines that it looked like something out of a dream, but this dream was real and he was making a very real decision. Steven slowly walked to his father, he requested to be alone with him, so Elaine and Marie sat out in the hallway. Steven went up to his father and looked at him with blurry eyes. He wiped away his tears so he could see his father better. His father's face looked green and his eyes were closed. Steven could smell his father's skin and how it smelled rotted. Steven leaned over and kissed his father on the forehead and noticed how cold it was against his lips. All Steven could say was, "I'm sorry Dad for not being there for you," then he walked out of the room and looked at the doctor and nodded his head. From the distance, he heard the machine flat line, it was over in seconds.

Yet another year passed and Steven finished college and married Marie. Joe did not have a will but, since Steven was the son, everything was left to him. He inherited the house and his father's savings. His father had a very sizable amount in savings and was surprised to see that his dad had saved up nearly ninety thousand dollars throughout the years. Steven convinced Marie to let his mother live with them in the house, because Steven did not think his mother would be able to take care of herself, since his father was gone. He was afraid that she would be a danger to herself or to others if she had an episode and he would not be able to forgive himself, if something happened to her or to someone else.

It didn't take much to convince Marie, in fact she was thinking the same thing. What Marie had not told Steven at the time was that when Joe was dying, Marie told Joe that she would take care of Steven and Elaine and to not worry about them. She eventually told Steven about what she said to Joe and Steven was very grateful to his wife. It showed that she really did care for him and his family and showed how much of a caring soul she really did have. Besides, Marie enjoyed having Elaine living with them, because she helped keep the house clean and cooked. Since Marie was busy still working night shifts, she was able to sleep during the days, without worrying about the house.

Steven, during the time, had been applying to schools for his MFA. He decided that he would likely have to get it online, which fortunately for him, online MFAs in creative writing were slowly starting to pop up. Steven did find a part time job as an editor for a small, online magazine and made enough to help pay for some extra bills that Marie could not cover. Steven would have liked to work full time but his depression was starting to take its toll on him.

The nightmares increased and, oftentimes, it was not only of his mom's episodes, but he would have the night of his dad's death replay in every detail. It would feel so lifelike that he would get up out of bed and check to see if his dad was still on the couch—that maybe it was just a dream and that his dad was still alive. But he would just walk into the empty room and he would see that his mom was sleeping alone in her bedroom. Steven was able to function enough as a part time editor, but he knew he would not be able to do full time, even if it was entirely online. He would feel the workload would be too much to handle.

Marie had begged Steven to get help but he refused. He would work his way around it to avoid an argument. He did not want to argue with her, he loved her too much to ever yell at her, and she never yelled at him. She would just shake her head and walk away. There were times she even set up appointments for him, trying to get him to go, but he would always skip them and pay the late fee himself. Marie did not know what to do and did not want to threaten to leave him, just to get him to go, plus, she thought that, unless Steven was suicidal, she would not drag him to seek help. She hoped and prayed that Steven would go himself.

One night, Steven and Marie were getting ready for bed. Marie was on her three-day-off stretch and they just got done from going out to eat together, so they could spend some time alone together without Elaine. They ate out with Elaine once a week so they could eat as a family and so Elaine would not feel left out, but they made sure to have their own time, just husband and wife. As Steven and Marie were about to go to bed, Steven realized that when they came into the house, his mom was not in her room. He turned on the bedroom light to make sure but she was not in there. He walked around the house and did not find her. He went to the bathroom and saw that the door was closed and that a small sliver of light was shining under the doorway.

"Oh, she's just using the restroom." He walked back into bed.

"Everything okay, honey?" Marie rolled over and looked into Steven's eyes as he turned around in bed.

"Yeah, I was just wondering where my mom was, I noticed she was not in bed. She's just in the bathroom."

"Oh, okay." Marie turned back around and turned off the light.

Steven laid there in bed, staring off into the ceiling. He didn't know why but he wanted to make sure his mom got back into bed, before he fell back to sleep. He looked at the clock and saw it read ten p.m. He turned back over and looked at the ceiling. Thirty minutes passed and still his mother did not go back to bed. He turned over and woke Marie up.

"What, what's wrong?" she sounded groggy, Steven was always jealous that she could fall asleep in less than ten minutes.

"My mom has not gone to bed yet"

"Well, maybe she is taking a shower."

"I didn't hear the water running when I checked."

"Maybe she was just getting ready." Steven laid there and began to wonder. Steven lately has been sleeping a lot during the day; when he finished his work, he went to lay down. Between his depression and lack of sleep due to his nightmares, he was so tired that he slept most of the time and did not see his mom much.

"Have you noticed anything off with my mom?" Marie laid there in silence, thinking. "No, nothing that I can think of. The only thing I can think of is she has been going to the drug store a lot lately." Steven sat up.

"What has she been getting, do you know?"

"I don't know, I can't tell through the bags, but it looks like a lot of small, narrow boxes." Steven got up.

"Where are you going?"

"To check her bedroom."

Steven walked into his mom's bedroom and flipped on the light. He saw pill bottles beside her bed. He usually made sure that his mom was taking her meds before she went to bed, but he walked over and looked into the bottles. They were full and the pills looked like they had been wet. Marie walked into the room.

"Found anything yet?" Steven grabbed the bottles and showed them to her.

"They look wet." She grabbed the bottle and took all the pills out.

"They all look like they have been wet." Steven began to tremble.

"What's wrong?" Marie walked over to Steven.

"She has been taking them then spitting them out when I leave the room." Steven said sighing. Marie could tell Steven was trembling, but in sadness, not in anger.

"Steven, it'll be okay, we'll get her help."

"I know, but how long can I do this for?"

"I don't know, honey, but we will work through this together." Steven looked around and saw some plastic bags sticking out of the closet. He walked over and picked up the bags. He took them and dumped the two bags on the bed. To both of their surprise, they saw dozens of pregnancy boxes pile onto the top of the bed.

"What the hell?" Steven said softly. Marie was speechless. Steven opened up a box and saw that it has been used and it read "negative" on it. He began to open all of them and saw that they all said "negative" on the tests. Steven stepped back and ran to the bathroom. He checked the door and saw that it was unlocked. He opened the door and saw his mom sitting on the toilet, with a pile of pregnancy tests thrown to the side in the bathtub.

"Mom, what the hell is going on." Elaine had her pants down to her ankles and she looked at Steven and then turned her head back towards the stick. Marie walked behind Steven and saw the sticks laying in the tub.

"She had more?" Steven looked at his mom.

"Mom, what are you doing?" Steven could tell his mom was mumbling something. He walked closer so he could hear.

"I am pregnant with your father's baby." Steven knew that his mother wasn't pregnant not only because the tests were negative but that his mom was too old, and his father has been dead for over a year now.

"Mom, you are not pregnant."

"Yes, I am, see." She held out the pregnancy stick that read "negative" in bold letters. Steven stood there and his trembling got worse. He began to shake and almost felt like he was going to have a panic attack. Marie stepped inside and talked to Elaine.

"Elaine, you are not pregnant, Joseph has been gone for over a year." Elaine looked at Marie and smiled.

"No, he did not die, he is beside me jumping up and down over the results." Marie had heard the stories of Elaine and had seen patients herself with hallucinations, but since Elaine was family, it was hard to bear. Marie heard stories from Steven that playing along with his mom was a way to get her to go to the hospital. Marie came up to Elaine and grabbed the stick.

"Congratulations, Elaine, let's go see the doctor so we can get this confirmed." Elaine picked up her pants and turned around.

"Let's go, Joe, we are going to see the doctor and run another test." Steven looked at Marie and his mother leave, Steven got up and crawled into bed, he did not know how much longer he could do this.

"So, it sounds like you have PTSD Steven."

"Really?"

"Yes, you have all the symptoms of it. The nightmares, the avoidance of hospitals, what you witnessed with your mom and dad, not only war vets suffer from it you know."

"Wow, I just never thought I would have PTSD."

"Well, you do."

"Ugh."

"I am going to give you a script for PTSD and some other

meds for anxiety and depression."

"Depression?"

"Yes, you have depression, Steven, which is one of the main complaints you had."

"Are they going to do anything bad?"

"You mean, you are afraid to be like your mom?"

". . . yeah."

"Steven, your mom has schizophrenia and bi-polar disorder, a very bad combination. Her mental health is way different than yours."

"And these will help with the nightmares?"

"Yes, and you will get very good sleep. You may feel a little sleepy during the day for a few weeks, but your body will get used to it."

"You sure?"

"Positive, plus if there is anything that does happen, come see me, I am always here to help."

"Okay."

"How is your mom doing now, Steven?"

"Honestly, she is doing great. I gained guardianship over her a few weeks ago."

"I remember you telling me something about that in our last session."

"Well, she has been placed in a good nursing home that specializes in mental health. What's nice is that it does not feel like a nursing home, she can come and go as she pleases as long as she comes back by ten p.m. or if she is with me."

"Is she doing well there?"

"Yes, she seems really happy. She says that she enjoys the

activities; she still gets to go out and see her friends."

"That's good."

"Yeah, plus she will be covered not only through her health insurance, but I gave her the money my father left me plus the money from the house after we sold it. I felt it was the right thing to do."

"It was a very nice thing to do, Steven."

"Thank you, Dr. Winsel."

"You're welcome, Steven. I am proud of you coming to seek help. We have made really good progress and I am glad I was able to come up with an official diagnosis today. Hopefully, you will be able to sleep without nightmares for the first time in years."

"Yes, that would be great."

"Well, I'll see you next month for a follow up on how the meds are doing for you."

Steven got into bed that night and turned around and kissed his wife.

"What is that for?" Steven smiled at her and touched her pregnant belly.

"For pushing me to finally seek help." Marie smiled.

"By the way, your mom will be over tomorrow for dinner."

"I know." Steven smiled and kissed Marie good night. Steven rolled over and took his medications. He pulled the covers up to his chin and then closed his eyes. Slowly he drifted off to sleep for a night free of nightmares—the first time in over twenty years.

www.ingramcontent.com/pod-product-compliance
Lightning Source LLC
Chambersburg PA
CBHW060542260626
47161CB00003B/1008